by

CLAYTON
ESHLEMAN

*CLAYTON
ESHLEMAN*

COILS

BLACK SPARROW PRESS

*1973
Los Angeles*

ACKNOWLEDGEMENTS

For the years 1962 to 1971 Coils was a work-in-progress called "The Tsuruginomiya Regeneration." The following sections of "The Tsuruginomiya Regeneration" appeared in magazines but were dropped from Coils: "The Book at War" (El Corno Empumado #24), "The Book of Barbara" (Poetry, 1968), "The Book of the Formation of Mercy" (Gnosis, 1961), "The Flyer" (some/thing #2), and "The Prayer at the Trunk" (Equal Time). The earliest version of "Webs of Entry" to be published appeared in Indiana (Black Sparrow Press, 1969) where it was called "The Book of Yorunomado." A modification of the earliest version appeared in Poetry in 1965. A very early version of "Coils" appeared in El Corno Emplumado #14 where it was called "The Book of Coatlicue." "Coils" in near final form appeared in Second Aeon (Wales) and Caterpillar #19. Section 1 of "Niemonjima" originally appeared in Tish (Canada) in 1965, and was reprinted in Stony Brook #1. An early section 3, now completely dropped, appeared in Imago (Canada) #4. The left hand part of section 7 originally appeared in Burning Deck #4 where it was called "The Water Closet." An early version of "The House of Okumura" was published in book form by the Weed/Flower Press Toronto, 1969. Sections from the early version appeared in The Ant's Forefoot, Rain, and El Corno Emplumado. An early version of "T'ai" was published in book form by The Sans Souci Press, Cambridge, 1969. "The Golden String," "The Overcoats of Eden," "The Baptism of Desire," and "Trenches" (in an earlier version) all appeared in Caterpillar. "The Bloodstone" (called "The Emerald") appeared in Tree 3. "Origin" was printed in Sesheta (Lancaster), and in Los. "The Octopus Delivery" was printed in The Poetry Review (London), and "The Left Hand of Gericault" appeared in Salamander. "The Golden String" was also printed in Earth Ship (England). "Mokpo" appeared in Hellcoal Annual 3. "Brief Hymn to the Body Electric" appeared in The Nation.

LIBRARY OF CONGRESS CATALOGING IN PUBLICATION DATA
Eshleman, Clayton, 1935—
    Coils.

    I. Title.
PS3555.S5C6   811'.5'4   73-1297
ISBN 0-87685-154-5
ISBN 0-87685-153-7 (pbk)

BLACK SPARROW PRESS
P.O. BOX 25603
LOS ANGELES, CA. 90025

for Gladys Maine Eshleman

(1898 - 1970)

my first source of power

CONTENTS

[*I Sing the Body Electric*]

I

My stomach was the sign to me that I was not damned, and that I was damned as well. I ached in my stomach when I would try to write when I lived in Kyoto, Japan, from 1962 to 1964. In the afternoon I would often ride my motorcycle downtown and work on my translations of César Vallejo's Poemas Humanos in the Yorunomado ("Night Window") coffee-shop. There I discovered the following words of Vallejo: "Then where is the other flank of this cry of pain if, to estimate it as a whole, it breaks now from the bed of man!" I saw Vallejo in a birth bed in that line, not knowing how to give birth, which indicated to me a totally other realization, that artistic bearing and fruition were physical as well as mental, a matter of one's total energy. I knew I had to learn how to become a physical traveler as well as a mental one. For most of 1963 and 1964 everything I saw and felt clustered about this feeling; it seemed to be in a phrase from the I Ching, "the darkening of the light," as well as in the Kyoto sky, which was grey and overcast yet mysteriously luminous. As I struggled to get Vallejo's involuted Spanish into English, I increasingly had the feeling that I was struggling with a man more than with a text, and that this struggle was a matter of my becoming or failing to become a poet. The man I was struggling with not only did not want his words changed from one language to another, but it seemed as if he did not want to be changed himself. I began to realize that in working on Vallejo I had ceased merely to be what I was before coming to Japan, that I had a glimpse now of another life, a life that I was to create rather than be given, and that this other man I was struggling with was the old Clayton who was resisting change. The old Clayton wanted to continue living in his white Indiana Protestant world of "light" — not really light, but the "light" of man associated with day/clarity/good and woman associated with night/opaqueness/bad. The darkness that was beginning to make itself felt in my sensibility could be viewed as the breaking up of that "light." In giving birth to myself, or more accurately, my Self, Blake's poetry became very important. I wanted to converse with Blake and knew I could not do this in the sense of Clayton talking with William, but that I might be able to do it if I created a figure of my imagination. It was really not Blake himself I wanted to converse with, but Blake's imagination which he created and named Los. The Japanese also see the stomach as the center of a person (in contrast to Western brain and heart). For this reason they have seen disembowelment ("seppuku") as the most noble way to die. I saw my initial work on my Self as disembowelment, a cutting into myself, leading to the birth of Yorunomado whom I envisioned chained to an altar in my solar plexus until the moment of his birth.

Alone, over coffee

— slowly, surely, carp turn
to a crust of biscuit,
nibble a kiss   in passing

Nothing changes

You, then, have been born; that   [Vallejo]
too is too obvious, luckless and shut up
and stand the street fate gave you

— ok, but
dangerously,   fully,   each
        is different

Incredible the force I felt in the Yorunomado coffee-shop. When
I first came pale sunlight was drifting a wide lobby open to a patio
where a tiny lantern's soft red, latticed, glowed. By cedar beams
hung with shields & by an amber table-lamp I took a high-backed
crimson-cushioned chair. A chanson played; out on the patio a
mother & her son sat down. I'd spend the afternoon there, trying
to translate Vallejo, trying to write. I could not get anything to
hold. But I had faith in that dead end & stuck with it

in the dark pool below
slender vermilion carp
motionless

love
grows &
spends in me

Like flaming voices the carp
shoot about over mossed olive stones. A foot deep:
Europe shimmering light, a wall with the intensity of heat
waves. But *this* brick wall, *this* crude
birth though something in me wants to wander off, to watch
a crimson pennant unfurling medieval sky —
this hand of bloodsmeared cloister wall . . .

O dimension of love I thought once existed, O structure
in which though terror drained no energy was lost . . .

11

Flame torn the voices roil in compounding fire
— no.
From this iron
chair, a pond of carp, though more
various than I first saw, rose-popsicle gold, plucked-chicken pink
with pus-yellow head, one smoky purple like night clouds
drifting the moon over Kyoto . . .   Blake's *Four Zoas*, Dante's
The New Life . . .

My language is full of dirt & shit.
Is it too great a thing to imagine
I can conceive myself?

— over there, motionless
          under the brown water-plant,
the one with ruby streaks on her belly,
pregnant — *who is she?*

———————————————————————

Now there was something raging
inside me that saw itself
outside me in the spider
in its web between the maple &
persimmon tree in the Okumura
backyard — a garden that yard,
when I walked out the door
I was in the garden of my mind,
warm beautiful flowers, stones
laid, a dry pool, the Sensuousness
of it all was upon me, but I entered
this without Barbara, I entered
Beulah as Blake was speaking to me
without Barbara, was there
suddenly in the outer creation
walled off. This was a new psychological state, or this Was
psychology, aware now
of wanting outer beauty, wanting to
rub my face in it, to be stung by
the bees & hot, to fuck & be torn
apart, that *whole* urge
that lives under my feet as I walk
in, pressing down in May sun
& the gold in a plank, lumber
resting for use, that
burned me because there was a life
now ignited that wanted
How many billion men have stood in
this garden sinister as its beauty
waved & there was no outlet thru
the pores, & I sought

12

something transcendental
since I couldn't realize
what a persimmon heavy rotted
off its stem, broken jugular, that
pulp on stone, was about,
was not just a persimmon fell, it
had everything to do with me
It meant translation I knew but not
simply one language into another
The man had to be there
Poetry Cid Corman was twisting like
a wire into my eardrums Was perception,
What did I *see*? I saw that smashed
self of persimmon
a pile of orange skin
The skin bust, pulp spills out
You are hooked on your own pulp, that's
sick, therefore not art
But I'm in the grip of a force my
body argued back, whose shape
I'm trying to recognize

It is Barbara who is pregnant & she is bleeding
Now I understand some of my fear

It is the fear of possibly never being born

Standing on sanjo bridge,

      the day grey, misty,
lovely, grisly, the kamo river
   fades shallows forever
winding out thru the southern shacks . . .

     below the bridge, in littered mud a man
stabs around in the cans & sewage,
& in his ragged khaki overcoat & army puttees
I was taken forward to a blind spot

     (he uncertainly
started up a rope ladder hung down the stone
embankment, reached the top & with his limp
burlap sack slung over his shoulder
disappeared down an alley
home? to his children?
              Who DO
I express when I speak?

Knives?   or Sunlight?
                                    & everything
that lives is holy raced thru my mind

                        Walking home
paused under the brilliant orange Gates of
                            Sanjusangendo, in
under the dripping eaves, cosy,
I noticed a couple pieces of barbwire
looped over stakes I had stepped
inside of

            the woman stood there

                    & then it came to me)
            I would kill for you

THE DUENDE

Overcast, after lunch, the sky
fled. A colorless darkening void
neither wind nor rain. The neighborhood
still. Walking, there was a light
around me insisting I must
molt more than my face, as if these
brown houses, the standing alley
water, were the only reality
I must change more
than the contour of my lines.

It should be that the smallest
bit of moss pearl-green on the old
fence occasions joy, and the old
man wringing a rag out over a pan
of water, praise. And when the man in
my mind smiles, breaking my brain
When he smiles I say children should
fill the alley, white clouds drift
high in the bright blue heavens over
Tsuruginomiya.

When the female principle takes over
the I Ching names it *The Darkening
of the Light*. Likewise it is
the point at which, crossing
sanjo bridge I picked up
faint, certain, a slightly fishy
sweet urine smell from embankment
stone, the scent of Vallejo

            I entered Yorunomado

14

                    sat down &
                    it translated NIGHTWINDOW

                    The coffee
                    breathed
                    a slender tea

open.

I lit on his spine

we Locked.   I sank
my teeth into his throat, his teeth
tore into my balls locked
in spasms of creational pain each
day I tried to work we Turned, I
crazed for substance, through him to feel
the breath of poetry, he ripped &
cried for food

A month passed.   He increased
I weakened & Doubling my energy drew

blood Not what I was after.
contracted expanding he was clenched
Being, turning mind a Dead Matter
Poetry eating at my heart — to translate
another.   I saw deep in my menstrual
interior a seed-pit, in April
I went for that, turned obsidian
to all other, for a month pent drew
out from the earth

cold, Vallejo kept his word
I was locked into his spirit which felt
the cold, thus I stillbore the cold, he
kept his word Spanish, I ached on the rack
of my own seed-pit, Spanish,
I fell back, another month passed,
a year.   I was wandering around
a medieval Japanese estate
the seed-pit in my hand.   I had

reached the dead end, but Japan
was no help until I understood
in the ancient rite of *seppuku*
a way. *camino.* on the pebbles I lowered

stonelike. whereupon the Ghost in Vallejo
raised before me, cowled in tattered
black robes, stinking from the birth
channel, he spread his fan &

pointed at my gut; he gave no quarter;
I cut.   Eyes of father, tubes of mother
swam acid in my eyes red amber
swiftly as one slices

raw tuna with shooting contortions not
moving a foot I unlocked Yorunomado
from the complex cavework of
Blake's flaming tomb, undid his wrists &

ankles chained to
altars of the creative sun.
This was the point upon which all
points turned

my contraries loose

    Set in motion the servants
washed down & raked the pebbles
In darkness they crossed &
recrossed, swinging smoking
braziers, chatting.   One picked
up a lopped topknot, dropped
it in a wood pail.   Far off in the interior
of this House a quiet sobbing
was heard.   Misery too
honest to be that of simply
a son of a bitch.   In the heart of the poem
there was now a real hesitation
before power.   The platform on which
the stuff was cut & shaped
this place
holds the life of another

      "Will you help me?"

      I turned away & wrote:
*I am taking a walk & holding Barbara's hand, a field
slower than centuries we have no mind of*

but Vallejo howled,   NO — LA MANO he dicho!

then you Barbara struggled up sinking
between your elbows, braced, & in your eyes
all the feeling of a woman who had miscarried

I reached in under the arched wall of your back
& with your help eased in under you the bedpan.

Kyoto, spring, 1964 —
Sherman Oaks, spring, 1972

16

TRENCHES

At the broken
obsidian,
the "fall"
where

man drinks,
woman is slop.
Original Sin
can be located:

the furthest
fallen is
the limit of
the "fall."

My identity,
Yorunomado,
is likewise
the pregnant

black

*

In the totem
our ancestors perceived
being depends:

I draw on cavewall, worship
the buffalo because I kill the buffalo,
it feeds me

I walk out on Ventura Boulevard,
billboards with ikonic bikini-girls, dead-faced
"beautiful" models

Men worship these twisted male-projected "souls"
because men murder women

*

"the other women"
he said, "the poems to
other women
are in a black
binder in my office"

I was torn between hatred

17

for that rot & compassion
for the man the fix
he was in, & I was seduced
for a moment to think
woman is a quality of
mercy in nature, you know,
a valley, a sheltering cave —
Then something about his work
opened, I saw the "girl"
in his net of lust at 3rd Avenue & 7th Street
near noon on a wintery morning to
find her on her back, knees raised, in
a snowdrift   smiling
                          up at him —

I kept thinking of that black
binder as a trench filled with roaches as I sat
by this bedside
of my dying friend

                    *

Vallejo
his ass split open, numb, angular as a bony dog
in white priest gown
the edges of his mask-mouth
dark with laudanum

                    *

A negative is soul-destroying
A negative is not "the shadowed side of a mountain"
The contraction of perception
(this side of the mountain is shadowed)
into person (woman is "dark") is
or seems to be The
Negation — yet before
the mind of the I Ching
man was seeking to justify
his feelings that
woman is to serve, is shadowy (inferior) is
shit he deeply desires.
Woman gives birth. There is something
hideously repulsive to man because he
coils out of woman. An endless
cave. A horror of the dark
he must identify with the mystery
of his own shit

                    *

Vallejo in a café, watching roaches crawl
out of his dinner

18

*

Over a trench crouched
teeth raised to heaven
      I discover new   But to put it that way sees
tension in my thighs   less than I saw, the coiling
                    black stuff under me I knew
in Kyoto enclosed   wld mix sun life — out the window
    4 feet down   in the brightness of light the bank
thick black seething   gleamed, the "volley" of trees,
  or stirred by clear   the "grappled" vines, this energy
gurgling stream?   meant *the power of conversion,*
          in 1963 I cld only see the bank &   bank, mound
stirred. knees   feel its strange compelling presence,   of Venus,
asleep straightening   I cld not get my shit INTO IT —   earth
up   small box-   cld see bank i.e., vine/tree contours   that
    window bright   as focus i.e., conversion, yet   without
volley of trees   the light outside the dark   any projective
grappled vines tug   water-closet *contained me,*   "size" I
        entwine   as a crescent moon   was stymied
of fields full of shit   *contains* the night —   before
       sprouting

*

Vallejo on his back, partially
covered by a dirty sheet, knees raised
giving birth
               Kyoto 1963 — Sherman Oaks 1972

II

The spring of 1962 my first wife Barbara and I made a trip to Futomi, a fishing village several hours south of Tokyo. Late the first night there I left our inn and walked down to the beach and stood there in intense meditation. About a quarter mile off shore was an island named Niemonjima (I have never found how the word translates into English; Basho visited the island and wrote a poem there which is now cut into a slab at the island crest: "Umi kurete kamo no koe honokani shiroshi — sea darkening wild duck cry pale white) — from where I stood in the wind and roaring surf the island appeared a black hump against the sky. I saw the hump as a woman bent weeping, and felt a powerful longing to go there, feeling it represented an aspect of humanity I could then only dimly make out — yet my longing frightened me. I began to dream that head-hunters were closer to this aspect of humanity than I was, and that they would get there before I could, and when they got ahold of it they would ·crucify it. As I continued to think about this, from 1962 to 1965, I became aware that my pain had something to do with my sexual energy, and that I was committed to someone I was not sexually turned-on to, and since I was unfaithful only when we were physically separated, most of the time I was living in a suppressive relation to my energy. It took a long time for me to do anything about this because I was brought up to believe that one simply did the best one could with one's marriage. The idea of divorce actually first occured to me on my wedding-night, the summer of 1961. By the end of 1964 I was living a dangerous state of internal divorce; it was as if I was an egg and my desire for whatever Niemonjima was was the yolk. Around this yolk was the shell of my daily life. The head-hunters were beginning to look like my old fraternity "brothers" and what they were after seemed more and more to be my own soul. I took the name of my fraternity, Phi Delta Theta, and an area of New Guinea called the Sepik Delta, and created The Sons of the Sepik Delta.

Reconstruct a state of seige. Draw his own hand.
Géricault on his deathbed, following the contours.

Daily by my desk staring out the window
paralyzed by what I saw. Garbage can. Limestone wall.

Follow the contours, fill them in. Géricault used yellow &
sky-blue watercolor, brown red & black chalk.

Bloomington 1964. Hot September sun.
Filled garbage can leaned against a limestone wall.

What could be in that can. Through the uncut
grass to the side of the garage I walked.

Left hand. Sinister hand. Unused hand.
I saw five deadmen crawling around the backyard.

Maggots carrying the spirits of the dead. My dead.
Ripe spirit cistern thirty feet from where I sat.

8 a.m. take Barbara to work. Drive back, write
all morning on *Niemonjima*. Read Berdyaev.

Solace. No work will further. Go to Berdyaev.
"Love is in no sense whatever the sexual act."

Camus. "Only in chastity is there progress."
Noon. Pick up Barbara.

Now my only lead was a woman I had passed at
night along Lampkin's Ridge Road.

A woman walking with her back to me on the soft
shoulder of the road as I drove home.

I wanted her in the car.
I did not want her in bed.

I wanted her in the car.
In the engine. Like gas.

Now I understood one way would be to
murder chop up and bury her.

That there was no clean
way out of Indiana.

But I wanted her most in that sense Whitman
spoke: "The chyle of all my verse."

I found
the words I wanted to hear.

Afternoon I'd walk to the Lilly Library
following the contour of the inward withering.

Thru a wide meadow. Under a tree. To reach
the Lilly and find *Jerusalem.*

Following the contour of
rhythm equals pain.

Expanding. Inward bulged pants. Driving
back into *Jerusalem* against a girl in the library.

Faithful life, life that withstands all torment
— false life! O false false mystical promise!

True life constantly builds &
destroys. Utter truth at 4:30 p.m.

Tall library window. Girl outside. Gazing into
my hope since the truth could not be lived.

So I did want her in the front seat
too, wanted to back into the woods.

Would I kill a person? No, I would not kill
a person. I would have to kill my passivity.

Maggots life
garbage death

To release an inner being
that knew nothing of death

But to pick up the actual woman if
I could & fuck her seemed to be DEATH

Why would fucking her *be death?*
Why would I have to be careful not to hurt her?

It would hurt Barbara if I were to fuck
her. Who? *Barbara?* No,

if Barbara were to *know*
it would hurt her. To know what?

That I wanted to get my hands on a woman whose face
I had never seen. Camus & Berdyaev

are fools. Desire
is not a metaphor.

O what is wrong with me
that my energies deny Barbara?

Return to what paralyzes you,
continue to look.

Literal can leaned
against literal wall.

It wants to be something in a poem, I can't
tear it from its look.

I *have* to find the meaning of life
in poetry.

"Barbara is fine — really fine. The marriage
is a good one" I wrote to one of her friends.

Window. Silver garbage can. Tears
gleam sunlight & stars along the lid.

7 October — 1 November, 1971

NIEMONJIMA

for Diane Wakoski

I

Yorunomado knew too well this corrosion — night after night
the fires of Niemonjima had gone untended
& now broke out in savage blaze across the island crest —
the altars smoked forth into the night. Who lay
in the secret darkness turned & twisted with hopelessness
    for marriage,
for the fire had been baited — twigs & strands of hugs tossed
to the hungry little flames — a log here a stone there —
forever! forever! & a moan went forth from the firewall:
A throw of the dice will never abolish chance!
To be redeemed you must go to Eternal Death!

Whoever stood on the banks of the Pacific felt the moan —
Niemonjima appeared a half-mile out black
against the midnight starless — flames
choked in mind — the altar unknown — no longer to
convert into the fraternity changes,
no longer is there a fake brotherhood of young men,
the savagery in the Plymouth, the so-called picnic, the raped pine—
& whoever stood on the murmuring shore stood
likewise along the entangled darkness of the Sepik River —
shields bobbed through the trees — the masks are prepared
that lead to Niemonjima's altars. For I am in the State
of New Ireland — as slabs of wood are bent blue white & red
    birds & snakes
across the inner shell so does my imagination
shake & tear against the roots & vines of Coatlicue's web of
desire & longing — the beloved unknown,
desired, but desired as a shadow dancing on Niemonjima's
    altar walls.

I stand rooted to these shores & watch the Men of the Sepik
(were they as mild as New Ireland!) move along the high
dorsal ridge, a half mile off shore, Niemonjima, her hair
crawled through by men with spears & bullroarers — her trees
    silent
to the vast Pacific; Niemonjima, beloved of Yorunomado,
why do I desire you & not her to whom I am wed?

And this is the problem of the naming (all things relate) —
whoever stands on the shore is without name (this is the madness
    that is eating at me) —
Yorunomado is the imagination through whose acts I make the
    images of
Niemonjima my soul, outwardly an emanation, but
these things do not exist unless eternal

26

& this is the problem of the naming, for within me
there is no name nor mobility. I was on that shore —
I saw Niemonjima & felt the consolations of Barbara
but who says this now? Through whom does this hand write?
Yorunomado felt his brain move off as if divided
by waters, as a sand-castle crumbles in surf,
O beloved Yorunomado, whom I must express, whose adventures
with Niemonjima are the life wherein I live,
O beloved Yorunomado who may not exist! This is the problem
of the naming, this is my love poem in these dreadful nights!

　　And I bowed to the waters miles below my hands:
O that the poem fulfilled my obligations!
O that Barbara were not my wife!

　　A dark wind moved in across the roar
begging understanding: the ways of women are most
treacherous to men only if man commit that
treachery first — for man thinks he creates woman,
because he thinks this he then casts her away,
& the wind wept in her pale tulle before him,
"So am I doomed to wander for the emanations of men
all waters in search of their lost children, I am that
confusion between child & emanation, I must wander
until men & women understand sexual energy must not
be fettered by creation. Terrible the drain on friendship
when blood does not division, when the parent-
power is not overthrown & Niemonjima sleeps in
darkness an altar at an island crest. Between you
& your belovéd has come a wife — before you were not
one, but now you are three! There is a Sepik River
in every man, of blood & shit, runs along his back
like a shrimp's." And I saw her webby skin, she howled
& was gone. O praise the Poetic Genius made manifest
in the 7th Book of Zoas: *Thou art but a form & organ of life,
& of thyself art nothing, being Created Continually by
Mercy & Love divine.*

　　I have opened a center, & it is this center that moves
confidence in these words, that they are of others'
experience well as mine, for as the flames toss
against the midnight starless from Niemonjima's crest,
so does she lie awake a tongue of longing become less
　　than a woman
until at last she is my mother, not Coatlicue,
but Gladys, umbilical, claiming to be wife &
　　belovéd, terrifically close to the true
marriage, but now a mother grown young
& married at a masked ball — the hour tolls!
But the covering has grown so thin, are we not
known all along? The hour tolls! The Men of the Sepik
hurry along Niemonjima's outer lines —

27

And the spirit of Barbara followed me down to the shore
in the form of Jerusalem along the Arlington, she stood
behind my kneeling in worry & care, whom I could not
embrace for if I allowed myself to feel something I knew
I would want more, would riot in the fear & madness of
my own powers — I feared a wife turned
viperous with desire, the maw of Tokyo
a million red lights to swallow the wanderer
& on his return present him as a baby to the ladies.
She stood behind my kneeling, pointing
     with one hand back
to the inn & with the other out to Niemonjima,
& the waterwheel turned inside me a rack
toward Niemonjima, I would not settle for what I had
been given, but I could not escape, all my images fled before
the constant recreation of Origin! So slowly the error
consolidated & I prayed with my hands horizontal to the surf
Yorunomado, help me understand my sex,
Yorunomado, let my wife be the one I love.
     For the Men of the Sepik broke into loud chants
moving now swiftly through her upper grasses, around the
     concentric
dirt paths toward where the altar buffeted & smoked
a terrible pink steam of desire. Praying against
the water Yorunomado let me be satisfied with generation,
let me accept her without a robe, the poem is *a persimmon
falls*, my ears are locked to my bowels —

     And it was only the robe that drove him on,
a vision of the inland sea, which is called the Gull-robe,
gorgeous, of white feathers emblazoned with stars & moons,
the lovely garment every loved woman wears, of midnight-
blue & silks, in which a light streams for all who ride
away into the darkness carrying the torches of imaginative
love, the softness & precision of loved desire. But now
the Klan wears the Gull-robe! The sons of Phi Delta Theta
commingle with the ordered rhythms of the Sepik,
& who is to say she wears a gown? The Eighty-fold Boar
strives in darkness with the Daughters of Jerusalem
     along the Hudson,
he is far from Yorunomado now arguing by the Pacific
with the hopeless wanderer who would sleep
contracted in foetal anguish rather than go
to Eternal Death of wife & generation
through whom only will Niemonjima ever flow
a river in the arms of any man. Give me

strength for my labor — for even now I doubt
what I write in the very act of creation —
I see the sperm spurt, the Sons of the Sepik Delta
dance around her tortured altars, the blood
gushes, the poor wife tilts back that her ovaries

may drink, the trailer lurches, pets flee bumping
into cupboards & chairs, the smell of garbage commingles
    with desire —
she is absolutely naked, in her own Xipe-Soutine-red flowing
    on the bed, the husband
flees in terror to the bars, but ah! the spirit of Barbara cannot
    hold him!
Like rising backdrops he runs open-armed through her arms —
the altar smokes, gems congeal, a Fat Carnival Face grins
between her pillars where the red spider guardians have
    fled in terror — all is

shifting levels of literality & darkness as memory
crowds in — Origin is singing "Your only sureness is to say
    the persimmon falls"
She Is Absolutely Naked. Without Imagination.
And lo! She comes down to me, she stands weeping behind
    me on the shore,
& I will not turn to embrace him or her for fear I am stone,
Yorunomado saw his brain hermaphrodize, sand in
love with sand as she swept back wailing, all wanted in,
the stopsign, the mole, prestige, he shut his mouth
& threw himself in ice before her blazing pyres —
the blood turns to money, the mind to brain,
A Victorian Christmas Art Book Jungian Bride.
Under the weight of this shale Niemonjima could

hardly move, & the Sons of the Sepik Delta mocked
her tiger-striped bangs Crying Behold! If you know so
fucking much fulfill our desires, we'll turn you on with
dirty jokes! And laughing slung a bloody bulldick around her
neck crying Behold! & clothed her in burlap sackcloth & ashes,
taped raw liver in her armpits, tied a string with "pull" sign
to her dick & shaving her head Crying Behold the Golden
Princess of our Homecoming! Behold our Snow White!

Yorunomado's only sureness forced to watch was that the work
of the imagination is in the service of a true brotherhood,
my desire to possess Niemonjima darkened by the canal
bereft of nightwatch in deepest fidelity to Barbara.

II

        And Yorunomado stood in the howling bay, waves
lash & wail into the booming caverns; he looked
to where the ovens were lit walls & the Sons of
the Sepik Delta worked in flaming reds & blacks;
O Gladys Enter! he cried to the shadow at his side,
Enter the ovens & be transmuted to my wife. Or forever
die, no longer plague me with what I can't see, for I cannot
worship the root, I cannot carry the taro through the lines

of relation. No longer is Coatlicue visible,
but there is a woman enfibered in my veins, a hot
wet in my hand I have been told, I recall is you.
And here you stand a writhing molten red, a
beckoning mush to maintain me always to the fork
& spear, in housemother agedness, while the victims
trembling holding hands are made to bend over as before
the mask was built, naked young men holding hands bent
over encircling the blazing center, a double fireplace;
"Slaughter on Tenth Avenue" is picked from the shelf;
where a frat pin was fixed through a sweatered breast
into a padded bra, the furniture has been moved aside,
the revelation of her armor & chastity is at hand, the victims
chatter & sob, the semen begs release — snuck out
in the crematorial lavatories it sobs to witness the flames;
the rites of passage deep-freezed her armor keeps them im-
potent, they stand being victims to be masters later! The hi-fi
needle is lifted, the lights turned down, the corral-gate bursts,
the Sons of the Sepik Delta shoot out bouncing & roaring from
their brides; only a few are not broken; I am shouting faint
with disbelief from the negation of life that is Indiana "O
generation, image of regeneration!" The virgin-wife discovers
on her wedding-night the spur-marks in the sides of her
little husband! She turns on in secret fury! Enter O
Enter the ovens that I may love you! Be transmuted to
my kind, invisible, for I am in great error, a part of a great
& terrible error, I must go to Eternal Death. Even as I speak
     the Sons
dress up in swastika red & gather grinning to my left,
the ideals of art wait patiently to my right,

>   *Whenever any Individual*   [Blake]
> *Rejects Error & Embraces Truth, a Last Judgement*
> *passes upon that Individual.*

                    Yorunomado knew
he had found his wall, for looking down
he saw his thighs emblazoned moons,
his ankles suns, a starry midnight-
blue painted as if on clay across
his gut. He felt his universe flex
as he moved more open across the beach;
he had taken upon himself self-enclosing
divine attributes; on North Jordan
he had passed judgement on a girl from Anderson,
in Chapala he had mocked a woman hungry for marriage —
but how not mock? The natural sexual
activity has become anathema to man;
whom he faced across the sand was none
other than himself in any other woman
or man, & to act upon them was to act
upon himself, a vicious self-perpetuating

                    30

doubt, & in the arms of the Sons of the Sepik
Delta he felt the vein of Gandhi, a pure
stream in India, but he could not mock
the presence with whom he lived,
and he remembered Jung's words:
The source of life is a good companion.

He looked hard around him on the beach
at the sky & at the sea. Were not all these grains
placed by abstinence? Was not *everything* sand,
the tree, the house, a friend's lip, a bird, a
sunbeam, when truth is overruled by creation?
There is in the life of every man & woman a moment
Origin's watchfiends cannot find, that moment
settles on various pins, it may be at any
place & must be taken there, & he knew he
was really dealing with desire, that that "moment" was
the moment of desire, & if that moment is
denied, the rest of the day is dead.

So did he attempt to understand the Last
Judgement he was in the process of,
now he knew the intorsions of seppuku,
that who he fought to emerge was not
just a spectre, Gladys wailed in the cry
of every passing gull but she was not
his enemy, only he could be transformed
in the coastal ovens, signs were everywhere
but there was something he was missing
to make these signs cohere . . .

Forgiveness & self-annihilation were
surely signs, but in what act? He continued
walking. Sea. Sand. Sky. No
thing lived or moved . . .

Distant down the beach he saw a bench,
or a raised structure behind which
something moved; on 2 x 4s a box, a
casket from which a tattered
windingcloth fluttered. He approached
fearfully for he knew who was in the box
but not who moved behind it; he approached
the casket of Vallejo as a book is closed,
toward the heavy box of flesh blowing
by the sea, seeing a man crouched
moving behind, who he feared was himself.
Los stood naked with his hammer behind
the casket of Vallejo smiling at Yorunomado; he put his hand upon the beaten
lid as the wanderer approached, smiling,
for he alone knew what I must do, & he stepped

31

back as I knelt by the box in dignity. in prayer
to Vallejo. Los stood & watched,
& Yorunomado saw how those who weep in
their work cannot weep, how those who
never weep are the weak, the fake
sufferers. To be a man. That suffering
is truer to man than joy. These were
the lines in the heavy pocked face of
Vallejo, trinities of intersections &
heavy lines, a village of nose & eyes;
Vallejo never left home, it was home
he always begged for even in the taking on
of the suffering body of man, I stood for
seven years & looked at him there, ob-
serving the Quechuan rags & shreds of
priestcloak, the immense weight in his mind,
& lifting his rags I saw his female gate,
bloodied & rotten, hopelessly stitched
with crowfeathers, azure, threaded with
raw meat, odors of potatoes & the Andes,
& how the priestroaches had gotten into
the gate, yet the edges of his gate were
sewn with noble purple velvet & I pondered
my own course, what was in store for me
given the way I was living, how the female
gate in a man must open, yet the horrible
suffering if it opens & something else does
not open! But there was no cure or cause
to who Vallejo was, perhaps it was the enormity
of what he took on, the weight of his people
to utter, & I shuddered to think of Indiana,
of what it would be to cast Indiana off.
Yorunomado sobbed when he saw the extent
of contradiction in Vallejo's body, how
could he have lived even one day, he thought,
this was the agony in the lines, the fulness
& the dark beauty of Vallejo's face horizontal
to sky, long black hair flowing back
into the sand, and Los likewise moved bent
& rested his hammer for one day in tribute
to the fierce & flaming profile contoured
to the horizon . . .

How long had he been left there? Yorunomado
stood & with Los helped the casket off
into the sea of another language. How long
Vallejo had been here! His windingsheet
was entangled with digging sticks & stones;
they set the casket on fire & left it blazing
to the shore water. They waded back,
& their hands were streaked with flesh,
their legs covered with veins, in the

hollow of their crab-like chests
a heart was hung, cock & balls swung
between their thighs. They knew
what Vallejo heard

beating beating beating the seas of misery beat upon the shore
& the roll in is a woman trying for a man
& the roll back is a man fleeing from a woman
& the million grains are children the waves beat upon
& the men walk in the women & the women walk in the men
but this is hidden to most by the very laws most have made up
Each sand is an eye Yorunomado is an eye of God
Every day every man ascends Niemonjima
for Niemonjima is the arising the going forth
& every night every man descends Niemonjima
for Niemonjima is the hill the walking down to sleep
& Yorunomado prayed: be patient with me my friends,
nothing is to be held back

                III

I turned to Yorunomado, saying
Who are you, if not my death?

profile over my shoulder, oblique in nightwind to the crowd   [Tokyo, 1961]
a hundred yards off bunching the bus-rear. I had come
down to meet a stranger: why was he late?
I had come down to get married: where
was the woman I loved?

                stamping in the cold, muffler
tight the crowd growing round the fender, close
around my throat: where was the word to
not look away, to look in
to what they were looking at,
the looks   are all over the page

out at me   into the center
(collect yourself, you must look at her   .   who was going
fast around the camp, was Yorunomado in the form of dog
dodging thru saplings, picking up the glow, circling,
foolishly circling, afraid to get warm

by her body? where she lay? mirror
broken under rear axle, pieces of blood strewing feet
of the strangers who stood
trees   at the center of   round the edge of
the clearing: steel welded tires, a frame

it is a schoolgirl, blue skirt, legs of 12   go
no closer   await the stranger, stamp

33

& blow under station neon
                         bloodclot
where shd be breath,
cobblestone
where shd be mingling
a woman
where shd be   me
in her arms
GO INTO HER

do not relive it   go   without going
art talks to itself, is not art, is the mutterings of
man   afraid

                    *

Yorunomado
divine man
help me, go
to her for
I cannot

I am weak beside the bulls of her forehead
I tremble by the stallions of her wrists

she is all spirit
a chimera of flame
in my own dark mirror
that smokes with need
of her. Go Yorunomado
divine man

for I have sold all my cattle
I have been put thru no initiation
the rains do not come
fertility is a stick at the edge of the blighted crossroads

Yorunomado
divine man
go unto her body
into her liver & bowels
circulate in her hair
for I am weak
I cannot face my death

                              Bloomington, winter-spring, 1965

After I left Barbara at
the Indianapolis airport
I felt crazy; drove out the
cloverleaf headed south

on #67 for Bloomington; I had a week
before I had to start hitchhiking for
Peru, in Bloomington for the last
time, Bloomington suddenly in erection

clearly itself, the place my mind was from not
for, nor of, I drove south
for Daphne's, found her home with friends
Her eyes in the kitchen Her

sweet sexual hesitant eyes (Al
hovering) I called up these people Barbara had
liked, a Dutch graduate student in Comp
Lit & his Greek wife, Taurus he had

at Denis' party said, & I returned I do not
get on with the bull, they struck me phoney
yet she was a bullseye, easy looked frustrated
I was desperate

We ate out on their back porch, country about 5
miles outside Bloomington, picnic-bench
bothered in the heat by mosquitoes
He said uh I've solved all

my problems recently. I said How did
you do that? Well he said uh I was always
horny & cld not study & I finally solved
it. How I leaned into this question, this

Pound book open under my crazed library
eyes lusting off in the corner of the reading
room for something in under the skirt of
whoever was sitting there, That

was reading. Could not learn since that
was reading. Pound in his ABC did not
treat man for this. Pound
did not read Blake enough. This last year back

in Bloomington I had the wonderful luck to walk over
each afternoon for 6 months to Lilly Library &
read in Blake's hand *Jerusalem*. In color.
There I yearned for friendship with Robert

Kelly, I yearned for spiritual comrades, to be
at powerful ease with those men & women I
spiritually loved, Kelly
a giant boar enigmatically looking at

me from the banks of the Hudson. Was Kelly a
spiritual friend? Did he know something about
Mexico & North I who wrote it did
not? Why shd Kelly take the book

& never write again? Or not for six months?
Why shd Kelly my comrade hold
my book, its miserable 200 copies, in.
I studied Blake & Blake relieved

the literal beartrap of these words.
Jerusalem is at variance with the professors
because they struggle in generation.
Jerusalem is that affirmation the woman gives

with her body, not mother, woman with her
mind. Woman body/mind. But that wife over
in the corner of this room I was thinking
eating my meat on this backporch night

Indiana country mosquitoes, this flying Dutchman
who was to sting me I understood, who was
thru his own no good reasons to take the trap
off my left hamstring. I looked at this man

with mercy for myself & him in my eyes.
Why shd Kelly hold my book? Was I a threat to
Kelly? He had offered to *distribute* it. But before,
a two years before, he had offered to

publish it, then imprint it, then neither. Finally,
if I sent the books to Kelly he said he would
distribute them. Wasn't this the old snowball
Poetry no better than generation

home. old unconsciousness. what had I
tried to raise out of. why try raise. fucked
world. Cldn't Kelly *see* energy. When I get
frustrated the Dutchman was saying well I

you know what Masturbate. Hmm what an emancipated
man I thought, under thought, hmm about dumb enough
for me to cuckold. And of course he was
setting us up. She & him across from me pulling

at my wineglass with Chianti. Drunk toe touch, he
lurched off back into house bedroom 8:30 p.m.

There is no clean way out of Indiana.
One does not travel/walk out. To get out is
to break out. Now Kelly had heard the hammer
not Los he certainly figured hit again & again during
that Philippine luncheon spring 1961 VIOLENCE
Ring of fire of which I still nurshed
at the rim. At her rim. Moved over, felt her
tits. Can I give you an accurate report now?
Can I tell even the literal truth? Can I tell the
truth against the possibility of getting more?
For writing is erotic, each impulse in writing has
a gain of light or loss, either way, & I was so
stuffed up was shaking as always hiccoughing against
her tits, we watched thru the mosquitoes his closed
door, then grappled out into the vast Indiana night.

Into the front seat, into the bushes, like a gun spraying
around for the enemy, trying to get up under her bra
Not to feel her tits but to get up under her bra
To clench my teeth smile & get her loosen my finger up up
Up under the kitchen window nostalgic beam yellow
Yellow around her Red Abdomen
we were clenched in her red abdomen
Let's go for a drive. Ok she said hoping so
hoping he wld catch us, but he wasn't, so let us
she is thinking hot it up come back let him catch us
with our raw meat outside, let him come in on us
as we are shining red, & open, let him see me see me
Flying we were flying thru maples down toward lights country
road. Took her back to South Fess. How I wanted to dirty
that bed, to fuck in wet shit. to tear off
the garterbelts of Barbara. to make her eat
her garterbelt. her fat. her Logan port, that
Logan old cheese. to triumph, yes build fire
in her body. to eat thru her stomach &
make a hollow, a fire place, to feel in meat
FIRE PLACE, rot
vegetal dead daddylonglegs.
This looked ahead.
Looked beyond the painful meaning into what it was
meaning. O I can't she was twisting in under over back
sheets Our smell Twisting in our smell
There are two meanings in the flesh my flesh was
fleshing me, If you are still with your parents,
with Barbara, you are enslaved. How? You are
not sexually happy. This finally means something.
If you are not sexually happy you are enslaved.
Right? Can you believe that? Is sex strong enough to
carry Slave? Not God? Not a matter of me & God.
Me/my God are against something I want with my whole heart.
This want is saying saying to me you Are whole

8 October 1971

37

III

When I lived in the Okumura house I used to sit on a bench built like a window-seat into the back of the house, and look at the yard, which was a garden gone wild. One morning I noticed a very large spiderweb between the persimmon and maple trees, and when I walked over to it, in its center was a beautiful large red spider. I was enchanted; "spider" was an energy deposit, a power gift, the first connecting up of language to my body. Each day the spider looked a little bigger; I decided it was female and pregnant. But one day when I went out to sit by her, the web was torn and she was gone. She had made me see her as a focusing out of energy with fibers which construct the world. But I was terrified because I thought with her disappearance my vision would also vanish. It did not. The spider and its work would come to symbolize me and my work, the metamorphosis of my disembowelment.

One afternoon Will Petersen and I were standing on a Kyoto streetcorner talking. I was telling him about the spider and also about my consequent fascination with caterpillars. I had been bringing them into the house and putting them in a shoebox with some leaves to observe them. Will quoted me a couplet of Blake's: "The Catterpiller on the Leaf/Repeats to thee the Mother's grief." I was thunderstruck — who was my mother? The caterpillar? If the caterpillar was my mother, all of nature was my mother — and if so, what was nature? Up until then, I would watch a magenta azalea bush from the benjo window and it would remind me of my mother's red wool coat she got at Penney's in Indianapolis. When I looked at a caterpillar through Blake's imagination I realized my "mother" was a shell over the azalea bush, and that I was seeing neither of them but caught up in an abstraction.

Living alone in New York City in 1967, a year into Reichian therapy, I found that I not only felt directly my old frustration in living when I thought about Barbara, but a lot of tenderness and sadness too. We seemed like two children to me then, two little people living in the Okumura house caught in an utterly false sense of "growing up." Coils was begun in those years, and was first called "The Tsuruginomiya Regeneration" (see the poem called "Tsuruginomiya" in The House of Ibuki, The Sumac Press, 1969). My original impulse to begin a long poem was to celebrate Paul Blackburn's marriage to Sara Golden in 1964, but as soon as I embarked on that theme everything that was happening to me broke into the theme in wild confusion because I realized I couldn't write a poem about Paul's marriage when I was lamenting my own.

For many years I thought I had two poems going, a symbolic poem which was not complete as such, and my own experiences as poems existing outside of the symbolism. In 1971 I saw they were parts of a whole, and out of "The Tsuruginomiya Regeneration" came Coils.

THE HOUSE OF OKUMURA I

On the road up Higashi Mountain, in
Minami-Hiyoshi Cho,
    a house for foreigners
    fenced
from the alley
like the rest,
but upon opening
the sprawl,
        a large beetle
or
   cauldron, the House
of Okumura
feudal remains of ghosts
looking darkly over the gulch
family living in the basement
& into the basement, deeply,
into rooms & areas I never entered,
& lived over by
foreigners
       & foreigners in the front
(wch was the rear

        a large beetle
or
   cauldron,   the I Ching
says *fire over wood*

   the idea of   Nourishment

THE HOUSE OF OKUMURA II

was presided over by Barbara
the spirit of the place
learning to cook in the small
kitchen the dark Okumura women
gave us,
    was recently married
a fresh breath
  into the musty fangs
of old Daughter unwed
bulldog widow Mother
grandmother Ageless, maybe 80
& Otake-san
  Han-shan of the place
crazed laughing char-woman
worked for her tubercular husband
no-good son
boiled red hands
washing the dark Okumura linens
mid-winter washing-machine rattle
thumping the wall against wch my back
books & look out
glassed doors
  the yard a rectangle of pebbles raked
& weeded by Ageless
  at dawn her there, bent, kimono hiked,
white chicken legs, weeding

                a persimmon & a maple
close enough to be strung by the
pregnant red spider
    over a dry pond
      stepping stones, rocks
the tumble of Higashi Mountain in ageless
                     proliferation

I loved you.

What does that mean?

I will not judge you.

THE HOUSE OF OKUMURA III

Would sit
on bench
builded against house
with clip-board look
persimmon maple in the eye
I still have those notes
that go nowhere
say a persimmon fell this afternoon
smoke winding across blue sky
they are like Cid Corman
              with whom I have nothing but
                  everything in common,
now what does that mean?

A red spider, swollen yellow-striped abdomen
crept out in dew to watch her
trapped flies to enrich the web
brought a caterpillar into the house
learned tiny redflower name,
        as if nature had paused
& Barbara brought soup
I am so blessed
so much has come to me
say thank you dropping coin into
                      the monk's hat
thank you for giving me the chance to
give,
        anger over calmness, I mean
my anger over your shyness
force over the gentle
                  reluctance
duration
& faith in me,
the weaker by its steadfastness
fulfilling the erratic strong

    Why do I break into tears
when I stop to think
        what were you doing
when I was not with you?

        That we have never
          each in each fulfilled

THE HOUSE OF OKUMURA IV

fish set on the table

warmth under futon

hustling off to teach at . . .

    : the hardships of that house

THE HOUSE OF OKUMURA V

dark cedar
barely lit room
    washroom
tub in corner
round   of dark cedar
round   of her soap-slicked
fingers on my breasts
  or washing my hair
from the rear

      pouring a dipperful
over me.
in like two daddylonglegs
together

        to gather man, to
grasp man.
          That such a commitment
aroused by
& thru you
was a distraction
              from you.
You were making me feel something
I could not give back to you
then. There will always be

an image of tangled arms,
crossed ladders submerged
in water, of us

There is no soul whole
none not a part
A persimmon doesn't judge me

but the earth weighs me,
as you rubbed me down
I am so blessed

THE HOUSE OF OKUMURA VI

(a tale)

Began at Open Sea
Sushi Shop on Higashiyama near the I-
magumano trolley-stop, eating with Barbara
& Kamaike at counter delicious tuna,
octopus, redfaced sake drinker
invites me out American, come
drink with him downtown. Barbara
looks at Kamaike Kamaike says
he looks ok
                goodnight, I go
off with him Kiyamachi-Shijo
bar district more sake big lip-
sticked bright red-lipped hostesses
smiling in dark sweet tiny bar
Can't understand much
Time passes
We're in his car driving north
Says I'll drop you off
Then we're in the country
Now to Uji he says Let's have
more sushi sake I'll pick
up a friend
                Japan Landscape
Night
           parked in the country while he
yells his friend out of bed a young
guy learned his English when he worked
on airbase
                End up in country sushi house
get the owner out of bed to make ten person
sushi spread I eat & eat & drink & drink
sitting with from somewhere giant farm
woman hostess filling my cup too full &
beat dead tired
                at 4 in the morning he
drops me out front of House of Okumura
thanks a lot oof
boy am I plastered
                wake up dreadfully
hung over all day long that night is
Halloween
              & Barbara has a party for
her Otani Junior High English Students
masks Mori-sensei & Kamaike dressed up like
women kids bobbing for apples in the tub
great photo of everyone

                     Nightmare
at a carnival I wander into a big tent
look at velvet covered table with
huge steam shovel Gary Snyder
in the shovel-cup being lowered to table
to pick up gold coins with his buns

Wake up the next day still hung over
dreadful day rain
wander over to Yasuhara's place
he's not in old woman invites me in
anyway, watch TV
                     late rainy dreary
TV afternoon the program:
                     highschool saga
fat boy wants to make it with his thinner peers
great track day & him on relay team has to
climb a pole
                my heart goes out to Robert Kelly
I watch him struggle up
and
tears come. very strange. tears.
& I am moved & leave
now dusk
           still hung over get on cycle
wander-drive head out toward Snyder's
Joanne home alone

          We talk & talk
about Jung & archetypes
excellent talk how I like Joanne I
think as at about 8 p.m. I get
on the cycle head home
                              .

                    I think.
Turn off Junikendoori onto wide Nijo
very very wide it seems almost like a field
cycle feeling funny air charged
something is going to happen I think
& then weird feeling of no longer in control
& realize soon I will pass by the great
Nijo Castle & then know I am to stop
get off cycle & circumambulate the Castle
park & circumambulate the Castle
which is square & is surrounded by a moat
This I do

getting off cycle in parking lot now fully something else
for the first time in my life I am out of control

                     47

yet with it, out of it but with it

                         The Castle was the World
& I am to walk about it first North then West
South & home
    or to the cycle
which is alone parked where the tourist
buses pull in
    gigantic parking lot   like a stadium
I float off
must have taken me 15 minutes to fully walk each side
once heard kids playing nearby
thought: if they see my face they'll scream
A vision at three corners it seems now one
is lost: at one was Kelly at the top of a pole
swaying I was moved to compassion for all men
Kelly holding on like a treed possum on
rack of medieval sky-wheel
                         great heart of Castle
pounding inside
                    looked at the moat water
Joanne's eyes passing over stone
At northwest corner The Red Spider Vision
an enormous spider bright-red mansized in web
The Spider was the Maker, Artist-Craftsman
also Devourer, a Mother eating her children
perhaps the initial conflict of the poet was revealed to
me then Great Swollen World Body mansized in web
bagged there at unknown corner of two small
Kyoto streets
                 by the magnificence of the Castle
Great White Stone Walls reflected in moat water
at each corner a dark
tall Rectangular Tower
                      I had marched the Image
this struck me later
or had marched my Circumcision?
Nothing seemed set
but everything was suddenly game

Got back on cycle. felt a few inches from terror.
Cycle was an ox I was holding to its horns slowly
moving thru the streets of Jerusalem
Lumber store immediately transformed into Manger.
a few inches from terror. very carefully now
picking my way back
                      Stopped at a coffee shop
sat over Herrick book in deep blue light
another hour Thought of Barbara now late
then slowly drove the remaining ten minutes back

to the House of Okumura
I knelt by Barbara
She was asleep
     walked out to glassdoor
tried to write this down
Still caught in funny iambic fear
Then startled & really scared
Feared a brute lurking somewhere in Okumura halls
crept out to john   my shit immediately a lovely coral
then another gleaming vision:
     A white bowl filled with blood
     sitting in a barber's window

Got under the futon woke up an hour later
I was in bed with someone I didn't know
who?
          woke at 8
fully refreshed

THE HOUSE OF OKUMURA VII

(A Commentary)

I had not been fucking.
I had not been able to write,
both, for several months,
"fucking" not only as the act
but the Contact Artaud was Mad for.
How can I describe the Contactlessness
at the Root of the Castle? I was out of it
& my Being revolted, put me in
Contact with another Order.
Poetry had begun to mean something, I was out
of verse up against my life Against biological
energy that if not allowed Out interferes
with thought. This was the experience of my life
to this point, to know that the world is Mental
There is no such thing as *objective reality*
The world we are begins in our biology
before we are born, but that birth is
as nothing Poetry is all about being reborn
Fucking keeps us flowing
If we stop forces riot over which
we have no control

Blake: "War is Energy Enslaved"
O sweet sweet Revolution!
                             That Barbara was
sleeping all those years — that
I was asleep too, that
something wrenched
me from my sleep!
It is our dormancy
repeats us into our mother grief!
Virtually every time I think of Barbara over
those years I see her sleeping
As if she was asleep to nest me
As if those years another was to be
dormant that I might break free

Sacrifice.
Bedrock.
No — if there is no objective reality
  there is no bedrock
    There are the 3 Okumura Women
a Kotatsu
          red Aoki flowers
unpainted Bookstand
Barbara's Nylon Panties

A Quilt   An Egg
    All these *are* forms of energy
seen from afar
  Up close they have a human face:

    I saw Blake in a blaze of fire
in night sky
as one afternoon I picked a caterpillar
from its leaf,

    He said, All men are under this charge
Energy is the only life & is of the body
I did not live
this charge out

    I denied nature
& affirmed it,
for I knew more
than I lived

    I should have left
Catherine
I was instructed to
My Christianity denied it

    Therefore I had to ask
Milton to descend
redeem his (my)
Female Portion for us

    Men
Kill
because they
live

    with Women
who do
Not
turn them on,

    I am that
Satan.
Don't
You

New York City, January, 1968

IV

Wilhelm Reich's thought as well as the therapy he had developed concentrated my energy on my body which I had neglected all my life. This concentration, in regard to Coils, began to bring the poem more into the present. When I was living against my energy my relation to poetry had been one, essentially, of re-vision; that is, because of blocked energy I distrusted first-seeing, and depended on re-seeing, re-vision, to complete anything. The most important thing I have learned from Reich is that once I was willing to go in the direction my physical energies wanted to go in, and once I was willing to assume responsibility for them, poetry ceased to be at odds with my life. The more I trusted my life the more I trusted my imagination. Life and imagination make up "the creative process." It took me a long time to realize that sexual openness means the ability to maintain a balanced energy-household. People associate sex with death because of an inability in their own personal lives to discharge enough energy. A person can understand that love-making is only occasionally an act of generation yet still maintain the old death-sex theory (which is crippling to imaginative activity) because the undischarged energy sours in the organism and infects desire.

In 1968, when the experiences and writing of the fourth section of Coils took place, I was still living out the shreds of my reaction to Indiana; I was like an animal that has succeeded in uprooting the stakes that hold the trap to the ground, but is still dragging the trap around. The trap of Indiana is: one has no body. The first stage of my escape depended on realizing and living out the fact that I did have a body and how I felt it conditioned everything I did. I became obsessed with this change of fortune, and for a time I thought that to be rid of Indiana was to be free, that fucking was a kind of end in itself. But orgasm is and, more importantly, is not an end. For an artist the function of the orgasm (in contrast to ejaculation) is to fertilize imagination and create an aura around the vision to protect the vision from the incessant gnawing of the experiential world.

(1)

London fog over Thompkin's Square Park
10:30 Saturday night
walking to unknown party
next week her old lover returns

9 March, 1968

(2)

to meet her old
boyfriend
lover
friend
  in her hall

dispersed

human

        14 April

(3)   APRIL LETTER

Marie, the sunlight's out in the trees —
colors in the skies —
   I'm writing you on the table where we
drank our iced cocoas
            winter is through
  spring blows
skirts   little babies
    are unfurling in the mud
the caterpillar
   the gnat   in lovely fairy forms
  are smiling in the woods.
  Clouds
pass over Greenwich Village — over your
      place on crowded Bleeker
  a fall & a winter I've known you
suddenly spring is so in the air
   my eyes moist wanting you
  make me pause
         grief is the only pause
   eyes clear no pause
      air spreads out thru the city like a fan
like the Kamo River in Kyoto you've never seen —

  Marie, so little, so
     fairy goddess
touched me with her wand
        waning moon my equinoctial life
   bruised moon of Clayton coming clear

  Marie, the sunlight is everywhere
   the earth allows us pass
illuminate the moon
   the trees & mighty river of our flowing
under a little bridge
   your fairy   beside the larger world
   your fairy
        keeping watch on your toes
  your very life
my tempest has wanted out

     today my thunder is in love with your raindrops
blowing high Manhattan jeweled chill sky
     Easter

57

eggs in grass
        my purple velvet touches
    you respond with the sterling silver of your glance —

Marie,
    the trees are walking like lovers in my
                    spiritual imagination —
    beavers come upon the shore, in love
with the wood they greet the mice,
        the bees, asters & the daffodils
                        Marie
        the flowers the hills are singing
        the hooded gesture of a violet no longer covert
            converted bright-purple
the cornflowers   sprigs & vines
        roll toward the sun their maker
in spiritual harmony my sadness lifts
                    All is revealed
green & glowing,   moist
        in the fresh sunfilled heart

April 15

58

(4)

O & the air
high over Greene Street
how this spring is around
a tiger capable of tremendous love

how this guy drifts up
& you open your door
draw back a garden of
pansies & violets
come into my rich earth

that you've known him
years, lived with him
four years, that he goes
on in your mind
                    no matter

the fact: I've *earned* this spring with you

        suddenly like a flower

        the plow shares

                    15 April

(5)   HAPPINESS

          receiver
cradled I began
to cry
          Matthew
looked at
me
     hurt? he said,
yes I said, my
feelings

are hurt
He watched me
hurt.

smiled suddenly
opened his arms
embraced me

I thought   I will
see her then, if
I cannot have
her commitment
I can see her
     Excitement
of dressing
Matthew,
getting in
the cab
that expense an
expanse, riding
uptown sunlight flooding
window Matthew
watching out my joy
his red sweater
Mighty Mouse sneakers

   & we entered in majesty
O to be here
to be alive — the Scientology
Offices where she was
found her, kissed
how nice to see you
how nice to be interrupted this way
  Her white leather skirt

purple sweater
Matthew

dragged out a Raggedy Ann

& Marie & I sat on the couch
kissing in full daylight

                    19 April

(6)   POSSESSION

I woke up this morning
       felt foolish
& thought of Crane's
    "Possessions,"
                over bread & tea
His fixed stone of lust, the magnet
to which he tells us
   all his filings bent
was an
        impure possession,
"In Bleecker Street . . ."
where you
          live,
too, where you

I woke up this morning
                anxious
& thought of Crane's
   "Possessions,"
                over bread & tea
His fixed stone of lust, the magnet
to which he tells us
   all his filings bent
was an
        impure possession,
but that possession
is a secondary thing,
anxious only possession
will give me relief,
to fuck you gives me this relief
to be anxious & think of another
     fucking you is anxiety
     deepened into pain,
the possession in the land
again comes down to a lack
of peace with one's nature,
that I was rejected by what's-her-name at
8, 10, & 12 in the poem seems
   like a lot of psychological shit,
but it's true this morning
as it's been for nearly two years,
Why must I again & again confront
my life — it is the poem, the woman,
   the meal   that follows.
I confront my body
yes, then

I woke up this morning
                    Anxious
reread Crane's "Possessions"
                over bread & tea

. . . .

reread Crane's
    "Possessions" over bread & tea
His fixed stone of lust
seemed the poem's "possession"
the magnet   to wch
    all   his filings bent
was, he told me, an
        impure
                possession,
his posse, his "after him"
—How can a man's power
be after him?
    if not in him it is
after him,   yes,
as this poem has become
possession, energy
    building up not
released,
        & at 10:20 I am stuck
here, the tension, to
        teach at 10:30

I woke up this morning
                    Anxious
reread Crane's
    "Possessions" over bread
"In Bleecker Street . . ." he tells
us (where too
    Marie lives)
His fixed stone of lust

. . . .

His fixed stone of lust
builds a pyramid,   or
    these buildings, the backs
of old buildings on Greene Street
from wch another building has
        been torn,   the age
in scarred brick, side
of Teotihuacan,
      leads to sacrifice
my heart cut out
        I say,

the heart of this matter so
fucking banal,
                    to be at peace
with one's nature
power
            not possession
at peace with my arteries
with the demons in the brick
the balance
at 10:25

I woke up this morning
                    anxious
reread Crane's
  "Possessions" over bread & tea
"In Bleecker Street . . ." where
you live
            Hart
at night being handed the key
at the corner of Cornelia perhaps
its weight his fixed

stone of lust, the small
man with beat-up ears
brought to that spot
nightly, as a filing, or

more, sperm drawn toward
egg, he takes it
he tells me, knowing it is
what he is pinnioned upon,

the release! the release!
men drink & die for,
Crane so easy to criticize
so seemingly weak his poems

open like hammered open
oysters

Open like oysters their shells
cracked, the sweet moist insides
standing there on Bleecker

failed in the twilight
as men cross,
    hats & steel
glass, the eyes' nights
a thousand pyramids

                I break
open to you Hart

. . . .

    failed in the twilight
as men cross men

. . . .

    failed in the twilight
as men cross   we realize
we never have the man

to possess oneself! as Crane
is shaved off in broad daylight

to confront

to let be . . .

failed in the twilight
as men cross
& it is these buildings
    as pyramids,   the pyramid
of lust in every brick of this world
men wear
        suits over their earth

. . . .

failed in the twilight
as men cross   we realize
we never have the man
he who enters our power

is but a phantom of
an earlier man,
who we slept & loved with
was our father
possession at best
    our veins are charged pyramids
every brick in us hurts.

the buckeye. don't you know
now how that buckeye feels?
And the wall of Altamira?
As Crane is shaved off in

daylight there are a thousand
others around you, the bowl

                20 April

68

(7)

What a night this is for Ed Iglehart .   he isn't home yet
but they are waiting for him
      quiet pot grower
or how I saw them, the bell ringing
stuck out my head
men orangutanging up the fire-escape into his loft
ran upstairs
Ed — ?
      Poking in my face Is Ed There? Sure, come in
Grabbed by my neck
thrust into a chair

So I watched them dismember his loft
these police in beards sunglasses pulling
out books, emptying jars, tossing Ed's
girl's Kotex across the floor

& was a woman, felt Vietnamese woman in
village watching the Americans move in,
overturn, these giants, so much harder
than my friends They are

granite,   their anger

is incredible,

they are breaking up the huts, pulling
peasants out of holes, these
well-fed trained to
the law

figures like shadows on Altamira wall
bison are they, bulls, with long hands

& that it is such a game   .
                              one of an infinity of
cops & robbers, their
stance: noise
at the door three
leap their guns packed to their asses
gripped, they
hunch by the door

quiet Ed Iglehart may be coming home

69

I have not looked into these faces
nor felt this grip on my throat
this queer nausea now
                              since a year & a half ago I
entered Reich's therapy, began to confront
my body, & they are vivid now
There is no shadow of the law
but rather hung-up angry men in a game
of wedge & kill

                    how Marx's words
hit, it IS not to just interpret man
but to change him,
                          rainy cold April day
I watch these foreigners move thru
my father's house
                          3000 years old in Nanking
Stockholm
                    you oughta see these hippies' feet
black as niggers
                          the crew-cutted cop tells me
This flying wedge man aims at Joan of Arc
Marx's words condense into the centuries

It is too late for me to study & become an Orgone therapist

but they say anyone can be a Scientologist . . .

                                          I wonder
in this failing early evening New York City light
waiting for Jackson & Dick Lourie to pick me up
go read our anti-war poems at Stony Brook

poem only viable if poet can decipher his Altamira
or this wall,
   as it comes now

          to my fingers' brink

                    24 April

(8)

These cops were messengers.
The truth is to handle this wall, this Altamira, to know
why
they are there, this long one with horns, these
unearthly figures
as if they were left there by an earlier race,
by another order
                        so far are they from the spiritual
delights of my
imagination,
but that they

are messengers, as were
the bikeriders to Olson opening
        the other half of
the beach, as they
entered with pickaxes, guns strapped
to their belts in back, over
their asses, tight there, to
black belts with linked handcuffs

were of another order
as from Altamira, in sanguine
rouge, traces

of an earlier form

To be handled in that they
still afflict what man is now

for to know them is to break
up the wall they need for their
very existence   .   Without

the wall they would not exist
would be so much
puddle, of water-colors, rain   .

As a child I looked at this puddle
amazed, which is to say to
the child their form is
dissolved
            Matthew would embrace them,
would embrace their spiritual being

would he not be so
put off by this game they've
so enwrapped themselves

in, & I have this coherency
this fine April dawn, of being
outside the slag, the rusty sideburns
one stuck on in mockery
of his spiritual form

That the true body is spiritual

That at last do *I come in self-annihilation &*

    the grandeur of inspiration   .

   The pose of that one
in black leather, arched
back as he perched on
a stool, aiming as with
a boomerang with his
crowbar at the door

   as he was coalesced there
a fine shower of arrows entering my
mind's vision
of him,
        boomerang
as the bull leapt over the candle flame

lines   driven
  yanged into

24 April

T'AI

the hexagram for *PEACE*
thrown two months ago
changed into TA CHUANG,
POWER OF THE GREAT
is linked with March-April
the second month,

I had come down to the book out of an absolute agony of purposes,
Marie was trampling
me under, I was
only a body, my being was
dependent upon her
love
          In desperation threw the Ching
stumbled into T'AI
not that I had the whole thing backwards
but that heaven & earth *were* in contact
would combine their influences
producing in time a universal flowering,
                        a stream to be
regulated by
  "the ruler of men"   (the law of one's
                        own being)
          which I know today is not
physical law,
              as if I could not
believe it then
& slowly sank back into the accustomed   .

That change come into our lives
that another's lover
                      come into our lives
that he stir us
            at first to possession, to
hold to that
thing so leaving us,
but that he come into our lives
inseminate us

    & the lilac burst into color, the rose
those flowers I stuffed
into your slot, left

73

dripping   April wind

Marie, that's why I could
greet Denis
& finally wanted the contact
with him,

all I'd feared had
come to pass
that another man would come

as I must have once feared
another would come
to my mother, feared &
delighted in such a form to
break up our family "circle"

how this fear lives until
another makes us face it,
suddenly we are
in the vortex,

as if belched up
so frightened was I yes-
terday before those forms

                I saw the physical world
a whirlpool whirling out its flotsom.
spars & wreckage of the golden dream
man is,

my name is Clayton Eshleman
was the name given my body at birth
I am not that body
I am Yorunomado,
                cave-scrawler,
    mocking up
my original
renewal of form   .

        I create myself

as you create yourself,

at root possession is a power,

a magic, to evoke

the miraculous

That the miracle is the only truth —
the rest is a kind of repetition,

    & I am taken back to
Matthew recognizing me,
to be recognized
finally
as one is & has always been   .

So I threw PEACE
& was shared.
The temptation was

to be sheared,
to create
my own leaving,

Marie,
the sign is you over me
earth descending
heaven ascending   .
   if I were to be
as in the past I had demanded to be   on top of you
I would continue up & away from you
   & you somewhere would be wandering
still in search
of heaven,
          which I now can offer you

The ruler,
the laws of our own being
   now divide & complete the course of heaven & earth,
further & regulate the gifts
& so aid the people

Let us go with this great ruler

           24 April / New York City, 1968

LETTER FROM NEW PALTZ

27 July 1968
New Paltz, New York

dear Marie,

I have come up to Jim & Carolee's in the country for the weekend; had intended to sit quetly through the weekend & at the end know what I wanted to say to you, how I felt about Scientology & how I would go from here. I have been talking to you all week long, though, & knowing what I wanted to say & do as I went along, & when I woke up this morning I realized I would write this letter now; I was so dazzled by the utter gorgeousness of nature here, the window on waking was so full, of growth & movement. Last night I meditated for a few hours at the foot of the bed; I had a hard time focusing on any one question; rather, my mind was continually moving & to sit & try to look at one thing seemed, the longer I tried to do it, unnatural. So I read a little of one of the out-of-print Reich books Jim has before I went to sleep, &, as I say, when I woke I was dazzled & again full of activity. There will probably come a time when I will want to sit & meditate consistently over a period of time — I feel for myself this will be in the second half of my life — now I see I don't want this, & the thinking I should had some penance in it for enduring so much with & of you these past eight & a half months. Now I see what I should be doing is essentially what I set myself to do a year ago in New York — continue my reading, work on my poetry & *Caterpillar* & be very involved with those I am involved with at all. The difference now is that I can do these things with more dedication & feeling for them. While we were together I often nearly lost track of *my* track (& at times where my friends were) — but being with you so intensely has put into perspective some central things about how I feel about the world — some things that I have halfway known or even fully known but, for reasons I'll go into later, have lived apart from.

What you have given me over these eight & a half months is various; you have made me sound many of my strengths — patience in particular, & persistence, ability to be put up against a wall & still work & not fold up in trying circumstances. You have taught me once & for all never again to embrace an idea that I do not intuitively understand & believe, & furthermore to reject an idea when there is living proof before me that that idea is functionally incorrect, *even if* the idea as such has great imaginative appeal. Patience is involved here again, as there are times when one must observe something for quite a while before committing oneself to it or judging it. You have also given me a sense of alive woman's body. The fact that we shared loving at the time we did, that you were the person I was with when my own body was undergoing changes in Reichian therapy, this means a great deal to me. It means so much, in fact, that I think for some time I over-estimated

76

it to blind myself to other aspects of our relationship that were destructive.

It's funny, my sense of you, as a "girl" — not as a "woman," which is too your sense of yourself. And sensing you as a girl (& as a fairy, or messenger, or spirit — things we somehow associate with adolescence) in such a way I never thought of as girlish, or without the innocence one associates with girlhood. On my part this was sentimental & speaks for so much that I didn't get out in my own adolescence or find out, take out, of girls then. You were a reliving in this sense of a past in me, of a past I was exploring in therapy, of a timid contact I had with girls in my teens, fearful to assert myself while at the same time I searched for the sexually most courageous girls, the ones inevitably with "bad reputations" to be in the presence of. There is this All-American girl image that was formed then against the very impulse I speak of above, for I never could pass over from my born-into middle-class world of dating girls who didn't put out & were (nearly consequently) popular to an awareness of what I had been born into by the way of sustaining contact with someone who was looked upon as outcast. I was afraid, & in my fear the All-American image was incubated & it has haunted me ever since, mystical in its power to draw me away from that which is truly sublime, the *other* before me. I know now I hate this image & would like to destroy it entirely — for it functions like the Virgin Mary or any chaste ideal, full of orgastic longing on one hand & asexual tenderness on the other; in *it* a man puts strength & love that naturally should be experienced with living woman. To have energy tied up in such an image (which certainly participates in "the anima" & that is why it is so hard to shake), makes for possessiveness toward the woman a man has identified with the image, for whatever of the mother is in it is not to be defiled i.e., fucked. The blacks perceive in "motherfucker" the man capable of breaking his own self-imposed ban, or man who does not long for his mother as he fucks woman, who can take his energy & give it to a woman without the split. What you insist is my "possessiveness" now, what I can understand is real about it, what is left of it, I trace back to an aggregate in which the local All-American girl, the prom queen, graduates into the national Elizabeth Taylor. And further I feel not only does this "image" have to be overthrown for a man to really love a woman, but the anima itself must be seen through — I don't understand this thoroughly yet but I suspect that that "image of my soul" if it is not projected as an emanation, or the body of a work of art, that that "soul image," that "dark lady" is the stocking man pulls down over the face of woman.

Thinking of you, the "girl" seems to me to be a point at which you arrested yourself in adolescence & have never gone beyond; that is, taken the next step into woman. That you are 27 years old means *something* even if it doesn't mean, as you rightly feel, that you should act the way American society suggests a 27 year old should act. But it means biology, if nothing else, & experience, & taking responsibility for, at 27, & not at 17, being fecund matter for the tribe, which I take to mean *creative* in the largest sense. Your failure to make it thus far in your profession as an actress means to me that you have still an adolescent image of yourself as an actress; that is, it is modeled on Hollywood in contrast to an image of yourself which you are forming daily through some vital contact with that profession you chose. I remember you telling me how dependent as an actress you were on others to enable you to do anything as an actress but I too remember Genet in prison writing on the back of brown sacks at night & when hundreds of those wrinkled things were stolen, beginning again. I wish I could get you to observe this — how you have yourself in a position in which you believe your creativity is dependent upon others. If you did observe this I think you would find that your chosen image has little to do with the present, for the truth is, whatever the image means, you are not creating in the present, you are handling your environment badly, & are obsessively busy with *manipulating* it rather than being in it & making love to it as you go along.

Our age tells in everything we do. There is so much of 30 year old woman in Carolee & Jim's house — in her drawings, her hand, what is set out in relief & what is shadowed, the boldness of the place, the physical boldness of 30 year old woman, the intense organic concern very conscious of itself, the books on gardening & wild life, the natural pepper that is integral to her art (which sadly so few see, actually see, *in* her art — how it is one effluvium consciously of the past 8 or 10 years in which there are a few central characters, worked again & again, sometimes as cat & man in the paintings, or man & woman in the notes, man woman projected group in theater — I mean she is not 40, & I fear it will make you furious for me to contrast you with her, but see past that, see past your cold snobbishness that night you saw her film *Fuses*, that powerful sexuality you called cold & unloving, for its counter-part, I mean the rest of the spectrum is here in this house, the basis of the fusing, the pictures & paintings of those two people which flow back into the film & show such a depth of happiness that one is simply convinced it *is* happiness & if so, then shouldn't one at least question the roots of one's own misery? I mean, not *rationalize* the misery or seek *explanations* for it, nor even seek to *erase* it, but observe it, say as a child who if recognized will cease crying & begin to participate in the common round. For you are miserable, I know that, & your misery did not end with what you have most recently done with it in Scientology, which is mostly a promise not to recognize it. In doing that to it, it only becomes more diffused throughout you, more mysterious, & *you* become harder & colder, for one cannot go against what one has promised not to do, for to do that, to open the dam, would be to say one had gotten nowhere with one's life & also to have to feel a great deal of anguish *directly*, to have to *experience* one's anguish, to let it come home, as a child, a part of one's nature which one, seeing it falsely separately, does not want to admit is oneself. But isn't that the first step in letting everything be oneSelf? That one's Self, that

78

center one can open beyond oneself, beyond the isolated "my," is one's seed (say out loud "self" & you will hear *grain* imbedded in the Anglo-Saxon ancientness of word). Semen. As a flower's "self" is its pollen. It is not this "selfish" closed shell-fish we make of it, nor a professional generousness to be given away.

Several times you told me you chose Geminis because you could control them. And when I was feeling good I went along with this — I enjoyed being controlled by you — superficially. I mean I enjoyed being pinched in the ass as we walked down 6th Avenue, enjoyed the sensation & embarrassment & the attention from you. But weren't we both, under this, a bit furious, certainly uncomfortable & always dissatisfied with what such control meant. I *needed* your attention because I could not naturally give you mine — for when I turned to you & expressed anything natural, an enthusiasm, or contact, such as kissing you, or rolling on you, it was rebuffed until gradually I learned to approach you cautiously & more cautiously at which time you began to criticize me for not being *yang* enough, for not surprising you. There was, simply, no way to surprise you that would succeed. I remember now the anguish you caused both of us after you would "return" or I would, having been away. It's hard to say where the cycle begins. Let's say it begins for you in always looking for genital satisfaction & never finding it — any to sustain you, by which I mean keep you in contact with one man. So we are separate & you fuck someone else. You feel guilty about this, deeply & not very consciously because you did not put enough in your last being with me. You feel guilty about this & you return to me but you do not say "I feel funny about this — uncomfortable about such & such & we should talk about it . . ." — for that would mean possibly you losing control over our relationship — I might get furious — I might reject you — or we might really find out where our relationship is at. You need the control at the same time you are stuck with that uncomfortable (& needed) guilt — so what do you do? Quite simply, you reject me! But not directly — not "I do not want you" but covertly, by creating an atmosphere full of tiny needles, of omens, where one cannot walk without fearing to step, where to touch you is to always risk you saying "go wash your hands" or after not having seen you for a week, when my first impulse is to embrace you & to fuck you, to be told you are tired, or a big thing is made over the fact I cut my hair, all of this of course having nothing to do with your *real feelings*, but since I can only be covertly affected by those feelings & am desperately trying to break through them, it is like throwing myself against a wall again & again, after which, after a time has passed, you begin to ask *me* "What is the problem, Clayton?" or "Clayton, you are going to have to learn to be more patient." Do you remember that night at Stony Brook at the poetry conference when I was so happy, so utterly happy to see you & you came in with a cargo of guilt & hostility, & I suffered through the day with you to the night at the party where you tried to run a Scientology "process" on me! "What would you like to tell me," you insisted. I had *nothing* to tell you! That was just it! And you had *everything* to tell me! But you reversed that & when I didn't "come through" (whatever that could mean), that was it. You were turned off, lost interest & dynamically speaking went to sleep, telling me I should not be so anxious to make love to you after we were apart, for it took you a few days to warm up! How can you stand yourself for such utter bullshit & deceit? What I have traced here is the cycle that makes men hate women: I am sure it is something of this sort that is in back of Blake's term "the female will." For there is such poison at work to keep you busy every moment refueling, maintaining, keeping a step ahead of whatever, whoever, you are manipulating, such a busyness that you never have time for what is primary: *to love & be loved.* Manipulation is secondary, it is not primary. And as a secondary there is no *true* satisfaction in it — only a kind of frightened sense of power. The beautiful thing is, a friend said to me, just how much satisfaction there *is* in love. One loves & that's it — not really "that's it" for "it" extends & plays into & among all of one's other forms — but importantly that is it. Woman says "I am satisfied: I have drunk deeply, I have drunk deeply of another's well. And now I will go write, or draw, or bake a pie or take a walk or just be here — I am happy — essentially I lack nothing until this illumination point comes again." Or to put it another way: one can then want creatively, can enter difficult tasks, can meet loss & unfairness in other quarters & not be overwhelmed by them but come through.

So, why did I put up with all that? With all that deceit & fakery that in therapy & in my own consciousness I had been dealing with & eliminating the best I could — tho not completely the best I could, for I just remembered saying that I would not give up drinking the night before a therapy session, & would go in sometimes hungover — that is, there is an image of myself very hard to give up that is balled up with not wanting to suffer my aloneness, not wanting to sit through without wine or pleasure the fact of my dying, the goddamned difficulty of gaining that inner island of strength that is not dependent upon the social. I have fought that all my life, & I still fight it. There is a powerful impulse in me to utterly let go, be drunk, write without thought, and coiling through that impulse is another powerful one, to be macrobiotic, give up wine, coffee, all excess, live monk-like in the poem, and I think Reichian therapy widened, extended these two powers, and it is as if they both tapped into you, you who are so flagrantly sexual & at the same time a little poor miser eating your brown grain of rice, or is it that I have associated sexuality with excess, which I realize today it is not, and study and balance with asceticism, which it also is not — or is it so painfully, stupidly simple that faced with being alone a night (I love to be alone during the day, I cannot stand being alone at night), I chose the pain of being with you over the What is it? Fear of the impotence of myself? Who knows what forces drive us into the arms of another, who knows whether something in us is waiting for someone, some parent to die to release us, or something in us to die, something we cannot manage at all but must wait until it lets go its grip, for I see how the 20 year old man is in the grip of the Saint Vitus of his biology in a way I no longer am, & I do not really know to what extent my being conscious of Self irregularly since I was 24 has alleviated unconscious prick to act. The great majority of men & women are genitally & spiritually dead but socially "alive" like puppets jerking here & jerking there, & I do not in my heart of hearts believe there is a mass resolution for this state. We are so ignorant we do not even begin to know what is in back of it, and all systems to this time are simply ghastly; they are like putting layer upon layer of paint on a board we have not the slightest idea the nature of, and this is a vicious circle, for that cargo of ignorance is also arrogance, & it drives men & women into each other's arms, drives them I say, and they see only the driving, only the being driven into another's arms & name that Evil, & some good fool is always standing at that corner with a speech to the effect that sex is evil, or woman is evil, & the social puppets soak it up again & again. In this sense there really is no evil — but ignorance, & ignorance is not really the same as evil, & so in our relationship Marie I can blame you & not blame you, can blame myself & not blame myself — there is that confusion because we simply Don't Know. But I will admit that & you won't. I will admit that the strong central suck of your cunt did something to my mind & body that made me come back for more again & again, & of course as I say this I see a spectrum rainbowing out of your cunt in which I wonder whose face is in back of your face, whose cheekbones are those, is yours the face that sank the thousand ships, what biological booby trap is in your pretty tight intense face? Something that was forever telling me *I am of one piece, whole, my reflex will be total, you can live in paradise without pain!* That I should have opened up to the extent I could become utterly led on by the promise of such mystical nonsense! But I was! That there is some conjunction in my mind that believes in spite of what I know that there is a paradise I can live in that has no pain — no loneliness, no suffering. Of course — there would be something crippled about me if I did not have a rage for liberation! But now I see that that rage is to be harnessed primarily into my art, that within the pattern of an art that rage can liberate, can be made, expressed, thus be out of the trap that otherwise in this life it can not be out of.

Scientology promises total freedom to the individual — to be totally free is to be dead, and death, living death is the end product of such a realized promise. There is no total freedom until all mankind is released from suffering, that which in the past has been called The Apocalypse. If I embrace any system which promises total freedom I immediately become involved in a terrible contradiction: I must be totally free sooner or later or refute the system & my membership in it. Thus one is forced to live a lie, constantly, if one is to believe one is totally free. As a Scientologist, having become "Clear," one is not to feel any more pain, one is supposedly released from pain & from the other dark feelings associated with suffering, forever. This is why anyone who criticizes Scientology is considered suppressive; for Scientology can only maintain itself, keep itself a functioning organization, by everyone a part of it holding their breath. The proof of the pudding for me was in looking at people talking, working, walking around the offices. It took me several months to let myself tell myself the truth, but the truth finally is those people are all suffering, I could see it in the way they held their bodies, in the fake smiles on the faces, in the tension constantly around, and the way any intruder or critic was immediately hustled out the door. Scientology believes that man is basically a spirit. This is not true. Man is basically an animal, if *base* has anything to do with heritage and body. And man in this sense is confused & difficult. But as Reich says, man *is* an animal capable of love & rational work. The lie in Scientology is to assert man is a spirit and leave it at that — there is no sexual stance or information in any of Hubbard's writing; thus, man as spirit is a false & unanchored statement; it is no better than any other crude doctrine which essentially hides hate of the body, and tries to get suffering lonesome people into an organization where they are made to feel part of some larger "body" by completely deadening them. Scientology is not very far from Sunday evening at Fairview Presbyterian Church in Indianapolis where I grew up, where the lonesome spectres would gather in a mockery of relation & pray & pay homage to a god like Hubbard who was never around. By postulating man as a spirit Hubbard then has to postulate everything else as a result of this, which finally gets him into saying that man created everything & is over 60 trillion years old, & in the context of the pressure of the organization, of the political operation, statements like these do not simply look corny, but appear visionary. They could possibly be — in fact since we do not ultimately know anything anything could be true, but this state of mind can only be handled humanly in art — to get people to act on subtle imaginative constructions which they do not at all understand the possible truth & probable bullshit of plays on & with the genital & spiritual deadness I spoke of before. And it was exactly through not understanding this difference that I plunked down $600 to be "processed" & thus entered my six months spell of Scientology activity. A curious trip it was, for on one hand I was wild about you, willing to do anything to win you over & prove my love for you, & because being in that state is being in hell, I had to constantly figure out ways to keep myself from finding out I was in hell, I had to, to put it clinically, figure out ways to maintain my neurosis; so the other hand here is being in a state of mystical bent, wanting to make a basic confusion, eager even to make it, to believe a mental construction was an actual construction — to believe an idea was present, active in the world, simply by the desire to have it active in the world. The thing that got me was Bob Thomas stating in one of the meetings you took me to that now, in his present life, he was able to put the world like a bowling-ball into a bag and carry it around with him. When I heard that, I heard it as a reflection of Blake's discovering in the process of the making of his poem *Milton* that all of nature can be seen as a bright sandal on his own foot. Blake says: "And all this Vegetable World appear'd on my left Foot/As a bright sandal form'd immortal of precious stones & gold. / I stooped down & bound it on to walk forward thro' Eternity." I think what Blake is telling us here is that through an imaginative advance he sees the possibility of a redeemed, or more spiritual way of perceiving the natural world, and he accepts the burden of this, and goes on about his work. But I did not have a good sense of those lines when I was sitting in the Scientology lecture; I was still simply dazzled by something I did not clearly see in Blake's lines, and it is because of that, and because of my torch for you that I accepted a cheap version, a cartoon of the Blake image as an actuality, & arrogantly thought if Bob Thomas can have that power — and by power I meant be able to have a mystical control over all circumstances — if he can have it, I can too, & it is ok to have because Blake said so. I elaborate on this because it is not only at the crux of the way Scientology functions but at the base of the artist's desire for fame, to have his power manifest in the world of his lifetime, to be a kind of noble moviestar, manifest before people's consciousnesses have been sufficiently raised to be able to accomodate the vision, and not simply maul it & use it as a club to flatten their neighbor. You never isolate a man so much as when you try to save him, for "to save" knocks the center out of relation. The missionary is a messenger who can *only* bring news.

I know now that in terms of therapeutical value the two years I spent in Reichian therapy enabled me to *alter* my life but also that that altering has not by any means stopped taking place, & that the therapy has opened me up to conflicts & energy traps that had I never gone into therapy I would probably be part of now but not be at times acting this part out. To release as much anger & grief as I did in therapy must alter one's constitution in as deep a way as the first breath of air a baby inhales alters his physiology. The 6 hours I spent being "processed" were interesting — I almost said "fun" — but they are less grim than that. I made some interesting connections between memories, thought out a few negative patterns in my life, but the main effect of that "processing" was to make me feel that you, Marie, lived your life in not only an acceptable way, but in an admirable one, and in doing that I began to imitate certain habits of yours which got me in deeper & deeper trouble with myself. Your coldness started to appear as coolness, and for the first time in my life the idea of "being cool" struck me as positive. So Jim Tenney came over to talk one evening & I decided to be cool to prove to him that Scientology was great stuff. I remember sitting across from him in the loft looking at him coolly & telling him how great our relation was & selling him Scientology at the same time. It was as if I was not there! And I shudder to think of acting that way — that I was better than he was because I did not show my confusion & hurt. This of course played right into your hands as it allowed you to control me even more. You had to face none of the repercussions of what you were doing. That is, you step on me, I don't say ouch. That gives you a weird delight *and* is at the same time deeply, absolutely, repulsive to you, & what is more makes you fear me (because I must be absolutely furious under all those welts), to fear my hostility in such a way that even if you wanted to you could not be free with me, not take any emotional risks for fear you'd get it right in the teeth. For if the anger is not open, woman always fears man for in most cases he is stronger physically than she is and has more murderous endurance, he will haunt her longer, chase & plague her longer out of the premium that he always puts on pride, his pride. I finally found out that in back of your treatment of me was a deep belief that men are sons-of-bitches. Either sons-of-bitches or pancakes. That was my ultimate choice: to either respond angrily & ultimately violently to you or to eat your shit & be your "brother" while you got your nookie somewhere else. After you taunted me that morning in Washington Square Park I finally threw my coffee in your face & smacked you; you screamed at me "I knew that was going to happen!" and sadly I heard in that some rockbottom in you, you knew it was going to happen because you were going to prove it, were going to *make* it happen — for the nth time you had proved men are shits. It is from that certainty that you wrote me the letter you did last week.

You said that you had finally given up on saving me. That you were releasing me once more to the world, as if I were some incorrigible child sent for the last time home from school. That you would communicate to me from another universe, as if you were, had been, my angel. All of this being said in words that were not yours but expressions you have learned through Scientology. And it hit me then, what a waste anything uttered is outside of *art* — I mean, how art is an *expression of life*, exactly, is uttered experience without that shellac of dogma, triteness, cliché, jargon that is the dead mouth of the world. What is that razoredge in man & woman that to the left of it just slightly we feel that he or she is not here, & to the right just slightly we feel he or she is. How pathetic that that seems true, that one is either *here or not.*

The sun. That the sun come through — I pray that the sun come through for you. For it is bewildering to be alive in this letter. I started a few hours ago dragging the sun out of the deep & it now seems as if it IS outside the window blazing in the oak leaves. How much of all of this is due to my having felt compassion for you, felt compassion for the very things that when I take a step back, or one forward I see in a pitiless clear light. You are little, the fact that I have loved you as a fairy must mean I am staggered by your frailty, that you are almost not here, & the razorblade moves, almost not here, compassion/disgust, compassion for the one almost not here but then compassion drags the sun of love down into its soft & snaky chambers & one is again grasping for the impossible love, O I know you have lost so much, have broken yourself over so many edges, have paid & paid for what men are, men who have irresponsibly put babies into your stomach & you in horrifying solitude & pain have had to endure your own inner flesh cut out of you, no man has to go through that, & is it because of that you believe you have never been loved & never will be, that you are Pisces absorbing all the shit in the world trying to purify it, make it spirit, is not that your rationale, & how can I ultimately damn it, your rationale that has you locked in a much more hateful system than any man you have ever known. And here you would say I am trying to pull you back into the muck, that in Scientology you have escaped what I represent, that I am looking out of the cave of my own inability to be free & obliquely asking you to come back & share my suffering.

And I just rub my head & say it is impossible, that I have lost. It is very quiet here now, the only sound is in the trees, the sky clear gray, a fly buzzing around one of Carolee's paintings. I know that I have lost in a very specific way because there is something powerful in me that would be with you on nearly the same terms I have exposed in this letter. I am split there & looking into that abyss. I must say that, for if I don't there will be a lie in this letter — I could not write this letter to you if I still did not love you & almost desperately want you, want to be with you at any price, and as I am feeling that terror now you are becoming a terrible vision, my vision of woman, my vision of woman as inflicter of pain, how I am magnetized to that stone, how the rails of my past point only to that terminal, & how I must derail myself from that drive that can never as such allow me the pattern I want to work in in my art. It may be ok for some, some may choose it, but I see it as an infection. And in that infection a face, a beautiful lure, the kind of face a man says he would kill for — not the face of sexual deadness that also drives men up the wall but the face of the inner projection of the social, the face poets have worshipped & adored, the "lady," cool queen of heaven enthroned in the ice palaces of the sky. How decent my mother was compared to this aggregate image that I have modeled!

I cannot pretend to know any less than I know even if pretending less seems to get me more. Last week I blindly wrote that sentence; I understand it now. It is the essence of what I have drawn from our hell.

THE BLOODSTONE

Where is there to go?

The more I set out
the more I return on

myself,
man. Everything I

said to you,
the opposite

could be true.
You
were my angel,

you will
speak to me from
another where.

Everything I say
fails in the light
of my tiredness from

saying it. The
birdsong stops,
the car

continues down the road.
I don't know
carries my conviction
I love you
palls before
you are not here.

I have my son
but more than him
my own tears at the

unapproachable
or The
approachable
distance

of everything I know.
A round
he keeps coming
back to me

I go over for him
a shower together
supper

but when I am most
with myself you
are past.

O give it up it
says, let

that lavendar
curtain fringe stand
for you,
let

him stand
for you, let
stand stand

for stand —
& then
you'll be through.

In deeper to
woman's love,
midway, there is
a field of solid night.

What I keep coming
back to is of such
monument

the wildflowers
field & sky
become my self

potential —
& I cease containing
I overflow

this house
in which
o & u
I encounter

your face,
sistern of stone.

27 July 1968

V

As Yorunomado and Niemonjima became more real, what they were not became more clear. The conditions out of which I sought to create these figures had to, as conditions, be created themselves in order for me ultimately to stand outside them.

When I was a student at Indiana University in 1959 I sent some first efforts at poetry to Cid Corman, the editor of origin magazine, who was living in Kyoto. A week later I received a response from Corman that flushed me all the way through as I read it. In one bristling paragraph he got through to me that what I had sent him was contemptible because I was not taking art or my own life seriously. I entered into correspondence with Corman and over the next few years he gave me a keen sense of the dedication to art one must have in order to make an art that is meaningful to anyone else. When I moved to Japan in 1961 Corman was still there, and I saw him often and absorbed a great deal of his viewpoints on poetry. As I began to try and find my own way in writing "The Tsuruginomiya Regeneration" one of the blocks I had to deal with was that because I respected Corman I wanted to write something that he would admire; however, in the very act of writing I would feel something that I thought was his presence frowning over my shoulder at the material I considered to be most my own. This situation held a double meaning. On one hand I was finding out that the kind of poem I wanted to write was not at all the kind of poem Corman sought for origin — when he rejected my poems I would be thrown into a state of doubt about my own abilities. On the other hand I understood that what I felt as "Corman's presence" was a deep layer of myself stimulated by what he was to me. What the poet Corman evoked in me was the stern father that I was to my emerging son-Self. In order to explore this area I created Origin as a master to Yorunomado whom in this context I saw as a dog.

In the spring of 1964 Barbara and I made a trip to Korea and spent a few days in the southern port of Mokpo. One morning we walked down to the docks, and my attention focused on a young Korean woman in a bright yellow kimono who was lugging a basket of kimchi (fermented cabbage) to dock-edge where she handed it down to a fisherman who in exchange handed up to her a bucket of dog-mackerel. Something happened to me in that moment: I can't desire her, I thought, but my God how big my desire is — "75 feet tall" I noted the next day in my journal, and I was fascinated by the unequal exchange between her and the fisherman. I felt the kimchi she gave him was worth much more than his crummy-looking dog-mackerel. I was relating to her as his victim.

The enormity of my desire for Niemonjima existed because of my lack of desire for Barbara. In a multple image of this double stress is Mokpo, which is basically the heterosexual dogma whereby sexuality becomes the lever of social manipulation.

---

                    appeared
gigantic on the darkened eaves
of the Senryuji Ancient Burial Grounds expanding
in the bat-shape of Lucifer
"You are a suitor — nothing more!"
the primal father called to Yorunomado
running around the stones below
begging for annihilation. & Yorunomado
crouched in dog (for the imagination nearly
perished he became what he was) & Origin saw
the chain around Yorunomado's neck
linked to the suns swarming spermatazoa
below the western ranges,

                    (take One)

Now I
walked up to Senryuji at dusk —to look for an
image of regeneration, I watched the sun
disappear behind the temple eaves
the sun is disappearing behind the temple eaves
flat, toneless, other images
spurted out, now I saw a pine, a gate,
but these dissolved into
what are you doing here?
was not a question of property
but you, why
are you alive?

                    (take Two)

now a man gave
me a power to see my soul,
this is Origin,
I was possessed by this
gift, was the Collar
of Yorunomado,
I imagined a man to be
free of a father,
Yorunomado was born in the wars of
Coatlicue & Origin,
Coatlicue is a force
Coatlicue is an imagining of mother,
having no mortal mothering poem mind
seeks its bedrock, seeks beyond
Indiana, beyond ethic a mother, a spider
watched in the yard fearful fortified
pregnant castle, ringed with skulls

91

devours its mate, goes as far
back as I can imagine, this image
inception of the second birth
seeks refuge in the mother,
is circular, the mother
is a temple at dusk,
will not come to form under the force of
Origin, Origin is the word
but word invested with
the gift, the gift of another's
mind, sits
a gargoyle
clutched to the poet's
shoulder, likewise inception of
second birth
I know is regeneration,
but in the form of teacher is
a soul life given, the son
must crucify the father

(take Three)

True war is mental fight
When one accepts a soul life,
accepts a princedom to a king,
when the pants are outgrown
there is either crucifixion or stasis.
When another assumes the role of
king or father, when the pants are outgrown
he expects to be crucified or unending
devotion. So subtle are these roles
men may spend a lifetime worshipping
a reflected power.

*

With this understanding the rudiments of the Sword Shrine
were glimpsed by Yorunomado as he stood facing Origin,
he took off the Collar & as a sign of humbleness placed
it on his head. Origin went wild on the temple eaves
& demanded Yorunomado reassume his former
position. He told Yorunomado he was not ready to
take off the Collar & in a display of understanding
published one of Yorunomado's yelps. How beautiful
the yelp was set in the darkened eave, a star it
appeared, an act of mercy, but when Yorunomado
barked & howled within the confines of the replaced
Collar Origin again appeared in the shape of Lucifer,
but then as a simple creative man. A friend of Yorunomado,
a good companion, who understood the barks & howls
were not poetry. Yorunomado was not sure & thus Origin
became his master, a household was set up, saucers &

pillows were offered; the image of Lucifer & temple eave now
seemed only a metaphor. For a year Yorunomado
lived in this pleasant place, his greater energies dispelled
a yearning always setting in as quickly dispelled, deeply
Yorunomado yearned for Niemonjima, a dream of a depth,
a center she seemed, that spot where battle flowed in
unceasing mental charge, the Sword Shrine; he would yearn
out the window of Origin's house. It was not too bad to
have a master, especially after the years of being lost,
& so deeply did he yearn the yearning seemed unreal.
Los continued to speak to Yorunomado that year,
often he would appear in a terrible fit of drunkenness
turning the lamp-shades upside down & overturning
Yorunomado's box. Origin righted these & filled the
saucer with cool water. But a disturbance was in
the house, for Los' constant intervention suggested
Yorunomado imagine what he saw, a drunken man
turning the pictures around. That the yearning was
true, that it was this existence was false. Again &
again Los would bang on the door at midnight claiming
the imagination was the inverse of this world.

One night he enticed Yorunomado to go with him on
the town. I'd like to go to Eden Yoru woofed. No, Los
smiled, I can't take you there, but how about the Beulah
Sukiyaki Lounge? It's a folk restaurant near the docks,
very reasonable with lots of sake & girls from Kagoshima
dance on long low tables while you eat. Well ok said
Yoru, but I worry about Origin, suppose something
happens to him while I'm gone? My friend, said Los,
your Origin is something you haven't even dreamed yet.

Meanwhile down at The Beulah Sukiyaki Lounge Kagoshima
beauties were serving delicious stews, & pouring sake
from urns & long low tables & incense & it was enough to
make one lose one's senses, a place filled with flowers &
dark balmy alcoves; it was Los' place, with swaying red
lanterns & a kind of steamy light & he entered with Yorunomado in a vision of pleasure; they ate & got drunk &
many beauties danced in tabis along their plates but the
vision would not forward because Yoru worried about
Origin & many beauties crouched around him in their tabis
with beautiful necks & he said to Los, I thought this was
your place but even the syntax gets screwed up, who are
these chicks? You seem to know them all & what about
Origin, suppose someone breaks in?
                                    And Los said: isn't
this the situation of your poetry? *Suppose someone breaks
in & Who are these chicks?* Isn't this what happens to you
when you write? If you can't be at ease here you can't
make it there; you turn off one central valve, you turn off
others; what you see back there you see here, only I'd

93

call that Ulro, I mean THERE is no one but you, like you
are alone, man, with a metaphor, & Los had a wicked
gleam in his eye saying To make this real you must make
something else real, which is very tricky but since you are
a Dog why don't you just go out & fuck a bitch?

Yoru was
beside himself, for the beauties got closer with every
word of Los, Yoru felt himself hot beside the fire of Los'
poetry & this was very weird, that language should make
him feel that way when the enterprise was he thought work
in his box, that he was a Literary Dog with primitive
feelings, & now he remembered the course of this poem
how he had plunged around with feathers & even donned
the headdress of New Ireland but wasn't it true it took
years to get that headdress on?

Suddenly there was around
Yorunomado a vision, in the ceiling of the Beulah Lounge
peacock eyes, the wood ceiling aswarm with peacock eyes
an arabesque of eyes upon eyes swirling gold & blue, it was
a religious feeling, of being in church & he fell back amongst
the pillows & overturned urns & wide-eyed beauties aghast
at the eyes within eyes swirling

(be responsible here, a
voice said; here you must get the whole thing accurate

&

at the same time another voice spoke; be utterly irres-
ponsible here, let the whole thing fly)

& at center Barbara's
face benevolent, warm, pulsing in the midst of the eyes,
enormous, as on a screen, Barbara's face smiling at him
& Yoru tried to turn to Los, but Los had split with one of
the beauties, or two or . . . Yorunomado was alone with his
metaphor but no, he was seeing the metaphor, but no, it was
real, & then I was not there, only Yorunomado was there,
only imagination was present, there was no division between
Yorunomado & what he saw, he was what he saw & her face
had in it Chinese eyes, slant & regal & long hair shimmering
black but a quality of turquoise, not emerald but turquoise
blazing in the darkness of her beautiful black hair which like
a mane was coiling & uncoiling about her face & furling
around her many eyes & her mouth which was pursed &
benevolent, kissing in its outer ceremony opened slightly
& he feared for his life as it opened, it pursed & opened, &
blood trickled as it opened, it opened & more blood bright
bright red, was trickling down the corners, now running
steadily from her mouth dark red blood & her mouth opened
now fully & blood was pouring like a falls, a terrible dark
red bright red, stream & in the stream a spot which was
suddenly a tiny face, an infant, & he recognized the infant
its curled foetal drawn expression getting bigger in the
stream of blood as my son & the poem flipped into constern-
ation as all this was true at once, Yorunomado saw his

94

son emerge from the bloody mouth of this mortal woman,
& as soon as it made its presence absolute the mouth was
again pouring blood & Yorunomado trembled on the floor
wanting to be away but knowing there was another dimension of
the vision, Origin suddenly appeared in the beams of blood
but not as master, not of the stern face, but Origin reclined
as on a couch, dreamy, heavy-lidded, his eyelids drooping
a heavy winey drooping & all around him beauties & Origin
winked in the bright bloody sunshine that illumed his heavy
winey form, & a shiver that this was paradise ran Yoru's ribs,
& Yorunomado shook & the vision like a veil shimmered in its
folds & then as suddenly only faint peacock eyes disappearing
as if stained water on the wood beams & Los was at his side
holding him, holding him on his shoulder & looking seriously
in his eyes, asking with his eyes are you alright & Yorunomado
came to, or it seemed, down, into the sense of his body, &
was heavy in Los' arms . . .

                but Beulah was not transfigured.
Los was there, watching him closely but as Yorunomado looked
around he saw the beauties in their make-up & saw their kimonos
were of linen, the dirty soles of the bent tabis, & saw many
of the beauties tending the businessmen of Futomi & Yokohama,
he saw their creased sweaty collars, their tight little bandboy
business suits & felt his own Collar, his mind flipped back to
that State, but he was intent on the women, & against the pressure of fully returning stayed with what he saw, the heavy
smoky lanterns & grease in the plates & he asked himself What
did I see before? Neither the beauty nor the grease, & in great
sickening feeling knew he had a son & that this son was not
a product of vision nor was a son of his master & that he had
had this vision but that he had a son, such was unbearable for
a year but Los was holding him in his arms & without speaking
they rose
              & Yorunomado in torment awakened Origin when
he came in, I must talk to you he said, tonight I had a vision,
tonight I found out, within the same vision, who I was, I got
drunk in Beulah, Los held me in his arms, I saw Eshleman's
wife & in her bloody mouth I saw my son, & then
                            but Origin
was looking at him seriously, intently, & told him to be off,
that this was gibberish, that dawn would come & all would be
as it had been, but Origin Yorunomado said, tonight I
saw the center of the flame, I mean you are not really my master
& at the center there is not discipline, I mean I saw you

                         but Origin
was getting incensed & making irate gestures in his nightgown &
Yorunomado tried to say I saw you secretly were drunk with love
& that paradise has no masters but the thought of his son which
seemed to have enabled him to speak usurped him & all he could
blurt out was I saw I was a sexual man, & this against Origin &

against the extreme complexity of what was his vision seemed absurd & he faltered & felt guilt for having awakened Origin & crept back to his box.

Now dawn came & Origin was right, he approached Yoru's box & speaking in an uncompromising way said: so you are sexual, so what? Of course you are sexual, but to explain the world out of you feeling you are sexual is so thin it makes me wince. So you went out with Los & got drunk: that is not your life, your life is only what you make of it where you are. And I have seen a particular look in your eyes recently & heard a particular tone in your voice & while I do not think you are malicious I think you are disturbed & I think you must work this out. I am not your father & the point is to tend to your poetry & lead your own life. If you have a son as you say then be responsible for him. Keep me out of it. I have my own life to live; you work out yours.

But you do not understand Yorunomado argued, I had a vision that I was a sexual being, I felt that the heat I am in is the heat of poetry. I saw my sexuality is more real than poetry, & that only if I am sexual can I be a poet. I can't live here in this box any longer; I must now go seek Niemonjima; I can't live with another's wife, though I profess I saw my son in vision & that that son is mine, but what a vision I had! I had a vision! You must acknowledge my vision because you are the man who understands me most.

And Origin looked at Yorunomado & Yorunomado felt shame; he felt there was something different about the world but he didn't understand why it was different. And then the whole business about the box & the Collar seemed stupid & Yorunomado cried & said I don't have a Collar but I do have one, I don't live in a box but I do. And there was no such house & no such master & in shame Yorunomado dwindled & it was as if he fell, & fell & fell but always a limit, a density, a kind of opaqueness in which Origin was most real, was his Origin but was Origin, & he wasn't a dog but felt like one, & he looked at his Regeneration & it was written by a bastard, & fell further & then bounced as he hit, & said to himself But I have a vision the way things are, this means more than anything & the vision is I cannot live with someone I am not fucking & fell, further, grasping at the railings of his body, & said But to simply fuck means more than the poem, the poem is a dodge for not fucking, & fell, more deeply into the density of what seemed the other side of Beulah, a sterile fusion of himself, & then he was alone & even Origin was a distant country & the only thing spiritual was his son; this flame a membrane against extinction.

Such is the nature of vision within the confines of the father & son.

19 - 23 February, 1970

the body
(Tharmas
never *seen*,
but experienced)
poverty
basically
body,

experienced as
sexual guilt,

devastates
mankind,
usurps
imagination,
one cannot
imagine if
one is that
body,

in the State of
Generation one is
that body,

the arc

of Yorunomado's
fall passes
through Generation.

*

Y falls
via O's
words,
a cipher

the past,
his own
suffering
embodied,

Mokpo appeared
docks of Pusan,
Barbara & I
came down

to, fishermen

haul in dog
Dog Mackerel
slimy

sunlit dockplanks,
Mokpo appeared
yellow kimono
in bare feet

come down to
barter kimchi for
dog, Dog
Mackerel &

wanted her, there
he first felt
what he thought
was Niemonjima,

urge
on the docks,
woman divided
mother

wife &
whore,
The Fates tumble
in the nets,

romance denied
romance
fills his pants,
Dog Mackerel,

the image charged
is cancelled by
its bulk,
Barbara

then, not even
a person, mother
then, a bad trip,
whore

his feelings for
woman,
Mokpo
the response

the dock woman
loaded the image denies
not just him, but

ah! Origin is

so close, Origin

is a man . . .

               *

flirts, he is so
coy, would like to
neck with Origin not
fuck

him, but that's where the
energy is, he
feels, & should
feel the shame of

this, how
turned on

to violence Clayton is!
A child, his
fingers spanked,
reads the Sunday

comics, turned on to
Blondie &
Skeezix, his
body neutralized, but

the energy! O
that energy is not
neutral AT
ALL. Mokpo

whose form we
finished creating
when we rammed
at 16

a confused girl's
hymen. Prejudice
become hate thru
who we could screw.

        *   *   *

And so in a very unchronological way Yoru left Origin's place,
before Los left him that night at Beulah's he told him he
must explore his dens, the density
of which, Manhattan, is a metaphor for Mokpo, which

99

Yoru understood was to seek Niemonjima,
he moved, with his son on his mind, to a Beetle Room
under the floorboards of Bank at Greenwich Avenue,
nightly he went out, engaging the talkers,
through the strange primitive alleys & bars, the amber
lights, turned on by Los, through which he felt a vision, to
find that woman! But in his mind she was Mokpo,
argument with men, a male ego in combat with what
it feared, for in Mokpo the feelings are hid, man seeks
woman as man, Mokpo is faggotry, man at war with
his feelings for man, who wonders why the woman does
not respond. Nightly he went out, a Literary Dog
with primitive feelings, Mokpo is not man's love for
man, Mokpo cannot really embrace (feels itself inwardly
a begging child), nightly goes out, seduces a passerby, Yoru
now yearned for Leviticus, Leviticus who was
an imagination but Leviticus did not call, Clayton
yearned to talk with Paul, but in the fall that must
get started a friend for his own perhaps problematic reasons
hesitates to call, & this is the glory of Regeneration, that
those who really do love us let us work it out, we cry
they would be better friends if they held our hand, but
those who love us know us well enough to not be, not
play with father, for the state of Mokpo as all states
is marvelous as well as terrible, it is a state of anger
& remorse, for nightly as he went out dear frustration
was there, dear dear meaning, that he could
be frustrated, for such is part of the birth of soul,
Origin as Lucifer is light, a vision, a miracle, allows
at its most minute sensing a brook through granite,
nightly he went out & it was the divine humanity
of what Los brought him to gave at least a point to
that arrow, he sought Niemonjima in the body of Mokpo,
something flashed in coming, something told him that is
truer than living in a box, to come in another, to go to
seed, beery anger of the unknown, politics suddenly real.

And so did social war, expansion of Mokpo, provide a
pigeon-hole for intellect. An aspect of Mokpo is reason,
if Mokpo cannot be brought to birth via seduction then
protest of man's horribleness gains cause. The woman
will be found within the covenant of protest. Thru righteousness
I will cloak my desire. Mitchell Goodman called me a spider
in the woodwork; he was right; I only fear he doesn't know how
right he is. I had to show Mitchell my State, how
could Mitchell have known had I not in amber light expressed that darkness. The real fear is to never
express it; to insist that Mokpo is just a port.

Late at night, after Yoru would come back, having
failed, Los would vsiit him, Los would light the candle
of his son & make him weep, Los alone would

visit him, The thing is so deep you will never get out of
it Los would tell him, This kept him alive — Los said:
I am with you forever, even by this flickering mortal
candle you cannot even enjoy, & thus Los *is* the mercy
of time, Los in love with himself slowly instructed Yoru
about eternity, that it is heat he told him, of first things
physical, that people work there, in heat, & thru Los he knew
his son was alive, through Los in that amber light Yoru kept
Niemonjima alive, slowly it came to him Niemonjima was not
a woman, this first, that Niemonjima was other than he had
thought of woman, & Mitchell Goodman appeared to him too,
always there was that very fact of man, who Yoru met in anger
but he felt what he was, Mokpo began to fall apart, Niemonjima became soul-work, Los kept by his side, Yoru now
sensed anew that longing he had known in Japan, to go to the
Sword Shrine which on earth was called Tsuruginomiya a
Shinto Shrine near the House of Okumura, there to sit at
night, away from Barbara to watch the moon which there
in its white obsidian knife shape suggested hurt & sacrifice &
woman, & as such that the sun was a man, but in the going to
Tsuruginomiya at night the moon became more a primitive state of
fearing woman, & Niemonjima was more the work,
slowly over a year he realized he had to abandon the moon for
the sun, Barbara's face had become the sun, had opened
within the folds of language an image of woman, that he
desired Tsuruginomiya not as a place of worship but as something
to create, to build Sword Shrine, to not project Mokpo onto
Niemonjima, Los insisted on this, Eden is creation, could not
be done in Beulah, Mokpo fell apart, became a book.

But what, Yoru asked, do I do with my suffering? I am
persuaded by your reversal of the pictures. I have expected
desire to yield the poem, that the poem would fulfill my
desire. Now I see I have never seen a woman, have only seen
my image of a woman. To build Sword Shrine is my work,
to uncover my selfhood layer by layer is also my work — to
keep that selfhood out of unconscious acceptance in the work.
But what about evil? Mokpo is real even if I was mostly
reacting to the Mokpo within.
                              Los answered: you personally
cannot stop the flamethrowers in Vietnam. You must do
what you have to do. To truly do is to be out of control
& still be with it. Treat everyone as if they are you, but
not your little you but that you with which you imagine
the world, with which you build Sword Shrine. Love this
Self. Know that what always interests You has not only
its source within You but is You. Beulah, Generation,
Eden & Ulro are what I can grasp of man. Be inspired by
what they truly arouse in you, *you cannot use them.*

                                    & imagination fled to Robin
Blaser along the quiet rivers of exile Vancouver, who
knew the poem, How can I deal
with this selfhood I am, Yoru asked,
Are you coy, Robin answered, for
the social question seemed to
press back on the man, I am no
longer Yoru answered, I have a glimpse
of a woman who is not my soul, not
my picture, her name is Caryl, yet I still
am not free to love her fully, I feel myself still
bound to the fear of my own powers, still bound, still born
to my manhood. You are in trouble, Robin said, & I will create
a space here to allow you answer. As a friend of Los
I know the distinction is between pretence &
imagination, pretence must be sacrificed
for imagination, the pretence that you yourself
are whole, that the power is real
in you, outside of imagination. At root
your relation to man, each poet
must solve this; you seek an answer from Los
& get sick in your stomach from the answer
Los gives, use forces you
back to Mokpo, man seems
to fall apart when you see
all your energy as something to be directed to
woman, This state, this
utter seeking is a deeper dimension of Mokpo.
At the upper limit of Beulah is the Covering Cherub who
sexually is approached as fear of another man, fear
another man will hurt you, your desire to love him
terrified that he will hurt you, beat you up, destroy you.
The error here is division,
social concern Versus art
has at root sexual ambiguity.
Mystery begins in doing something dishonest,
then you begin to feel
mystical — all systems are held in place
by a hermaphrodite, a giant hermaphrodite crouched
in their basement, a sterile fusion.
Translation is the passing of the bio-genital
into form. Blake
translated himself
into himSelf via Milton. You
do not have to
go there *to be*
              there.

*

102

Who was Caryl? She seemed to grow out of
the end of Mokpo, a dazzling lure, a dainty bull
in the clarified pasture. But was
she not my picture, my creation? Yorunomado asked Los,
& Los smiled Enitharmon, I am the child
he joked of Tharmas & Enion,
but this joke is a gentle laugh runs through creation,
the robin's song! Don't you hear
that carol as Origin quizzes you,
as all that has been your world converges on
you, that which you seek, don't you
hear that robin, that song
coming through the childwood, *Never
can the soul of sweet delight be defiled!* We are
all made up, happy in the reality of
our illusion, dressed as it were in
the poem, the poem
is the only dress we wear!
All we are is
our imagination. Be
here without coming
here the robin sings,
a not too subtle pun
ringing of creation!

But how can I lift this body that is now
upon me, Yorunomado
went out silently in the night
& sought a composite of the song &
Tsuruginomiya, a woman yet
a memory, he sought in all
this complex, the force of the bars drifted
into primal bedrooms
Yorunomado laughed at the words
to get fucked yet to depress
softly with a finger
that pedal in woman
might be Tsuruginomiya
For to remember her still
lured—
        Origin
now
entered the Beetle Room
Why did you take off? Barbara
is alone with your son. But he is my son
of a vision Yorunomado
argued,
        & I entered the poem
really for the first time at this point:
I must enter here I told him, I must take responsibility
for my part of the vision. I passed out in McCormick's
Creek State Park near Bloomington flooded with acid

103

& gave the stallions of my life over to you, You
Yoru, took them, but it was I
unhappy with Barbara longing
to be free of not
her but what I could not bear of
my own menstrual lining
made her pregnant,
Matthew is my son!
I could not tolerate this loving, I mean the love
I felt for him,
                    but this is a lie, Yoru said: you left her
because you could not tolerate the life both aroused in you.
You put this on me,
      & in the tender membrane of my argument with Origin
you threw down Barbara's torch.
You could not stand
that intensity! That in your life
which was stone you could feel
both time & eternity!
You slipt out
    through the mercy of Adrienne to
the Beetle Room.
I have assumed, have taken on, Origin's negative
vibrations to create a space for your body to heal in.
Matthew IS a vision, Matthew will know he is a vision,
& here I charge you
your part of the masculine flame,
that as father Matthew is your Regeneration
as man Caryl is your Regeneration
as poet the building of Sword Shrine is Regeneration
      & with one swift motion I saw Yoru grab
          Origin & slit his throat.

And then I softened & touched him, fearfully
touched him uncoyly wanting to touch him,
his side, the side of his face, & in no sense
of father & son touched his hips
& his penis, & we were down in the sea
of imagination, high
over the heaven of earth, bathed
in what the poem is,
he was flame to me &
I feared with my arms
around him to take him
into my mouth & memory then
became a nipple, cleared,
& we were on the spider-rug,
sulphur & crimson, the true
darkness of language, Mokpo the horrible
was a man, & Yorunomado
blew my mind without consideration, bathed in the
sea of a man, without fury, seeking

gratification Only an artery-pulse
from the Ulro, Only an instant
from the mockery of sterile fusion,
flame upon flame within flame
Wheels he seemed, as slimy
as I had dreamed Mokpo
the horrible a man Imagination
yet a man & he came into my throat
He entered my mind Mokpo the horrendous was
desiring man on desiring hand
& Matthew was an angel ventilating our desire
& Origin a squeezed second an elf
laughing & laughing while Los' beauties looked up
at us as if we were
that Upper Room, man
to be tried again & again
To live as a sexual being
with all I know of the spiritual world, to be
with man in the toilet &
man in the Okumura Garden &
with man in the auditorium &
with man in woman &
with woman in man
Mokpo the invincible in ritual
regalia appeared, in yellow silk
kimono with bucket of hissing vipers
As an animal seems to seek out
the hunter who has patiently waited
In ritual garb Mokpo appeared to
disembowel herself of feminine gender
to become an it to be burned as a stake
at the crossroads of the mind & heart
Keep away from this other man, fear
him argue with him This was her deathsong
& with a roar Yorunomado blazed over the hill
With Yorunomado I brought down the internal
whore Biafra was seen Vietnam the political
that could not answer was man's sexual dis-
comfort with man cloaked in the heterosexual
Viper A WOMAN TRADING ON THE DOCKS
her sway

February - March, 1970
New York City

VI

When I moved to New York City the spring of 1966 I was a cocked gun. The following formation occurred: I was staying with Paul Blackburn, drinking it up and once again ineptly and furtively looking for sex. One night Paul said, "Let's go to Max's Kansas City" and suddenly I was filled with the prospect of meeting someone there I would really like. I did, and as we were dancing upstairs I told her I had a baby son, and that I thought the greatest thing that could happen between a man and a woman was a child (Corman had suggested a couple years before that what I really wanted was a son; I was so confused then about what I did want that I accepted what he said) — Adrienne shouted back at me across the dance-floor, "No! It's an orgasm!" and what she said hit home. The following day I discovered an 18th century Indian painting (reproduced in Erich Neumann's The Origins and History of Consciousness) called "The Birth of Vishnu" which depicted a young man naked but for some jewels like electric lights mysteriously draped around his body lying on his back on a big leaf. With his right hand he had brought his right foot to his mouth and was casually sucking on it looking off dreamily and smiling. With his left hand he was playing with himself. The night of July 15 I wrote in my notebook:

> Vishnu on a leaf
> a caterpillar in the sea of a backyard
> eats his toe, leg curled
>   makes the circle
>   by which he tells us
>   — his other hand playing in his crotch —
>   his title
>
>   The Birth of Vishnu,
> not Vishnu's guilt   nor Vishnu's play, but
> The Origin & History of Consciousness.
>   How
>   simple that is,
>   all
> endeavor, creation, ballasted on the enjoyment of
> the body,   & I am 31 years old to
> learn it

Adrienne protested that she did not want to get involved because I was married (Barbara and Matthew, who was several months old then, were to move to New York City as soon as I found work); but I was at her like a person who had discovered a door out of hell. A few nights later we made love and I had a vision as I entered her of entering a bottomless well of cool water after crawling for years on a desert. The next morning I awoke after she did and found her taking a bath in her kitchen tub. I stood there watching her soap herself feeling that she was giving me the very heart of redemption. "What do you do when you are not with a man?" I said. She smiled at me and answered, "I masturbate." I suddenly understood that there was nothing "wrong" with my body.

Adrienne appeared to me not only as Adrienne but as Ariadne leading the warrior Theseus through the labyrinth having given him a ball of string. I picked up this thread as Blake's "golden string" and understood that "Heaven's gate/ Built in Jerusalem's wall" was on one level woman's cunt through which I was to find my own "Western path" through what for most men were considered "the Gates of Wrath."

Several years later, near the termination of therapy when "streaming" was making itself felt in my genitals, I had a very vivid dream in which my mother and father appeared as my friends. In "The Overcoats of Eden" I recreated this dream as the substance I discovered in Adrienne's arms.

Above all the kitchen bathtub with little white lion feet
where you bathe in the lovely shore light off Hydra

Above all the golden string

Adrienne
Ariadne
soaping your arms & wishing me well in the bright gladiator light at the
[poem's limits
which is but a leaf on wch baby Yorunomado burbles & curls full of play
This Self wch is flooded at the touch of your hand to the ignition

Above all
Adrienne
Ariadne
Above all Barbara who suffered it

for there is always a third who is there in the raw breakthrough of being
A third who stands at cross-purposes with our heart
wishing the antagonists well, the Holy Host

It is she who is pregnant with their desires
She clasps their book to her heart & waits in the dense Okumura garden
& Paradise is to admit her, she stands
before the lovers with an infant in her arms

This is the way of the earth, that the garden is always slightly off center
That the stallions of total translation are never loosed
Thus not an answer but a golden string is given

Above all this golden string

leads me to your bathtub in the garden where you are soaping & laughing
& your slippery happiness is deep
& great enough for me to enter fully & be bathed
in the cool
reality of the mirage

Come on in, Barbara!
Don't you know this golden string allows you & Matthew to laugh
& splash with us, that this garden is incomplete without both of you
entering the bubbles & rubies of all our desires
The pregnant red spider,

the flies, the cicadas in *The House of Okumura*
can here follow Adrienne's golden string & laugh & dance with us
in the great dimension of
this string

And this is the construction of this string,
it is interwoven with indignation & hesitancy, with dark
reservation & loss
For in vision these withholdings are the pressed
bodies of the creatures with whom we dance,
the terrible sun illumes for us the bastings of blood, the pressed

lives of the creatures, the pregnant spider abandoned
as the cold sets in is here, the pumpkin-colored slug on
the frosted October ledge, all the terrified captives

cut down by the gladiators in the light at the poem's limit

Thus the energy of my dream reverberates down the golden coils
of the imagination, this paradise wch is not mine alone fans
& deepens with the churring of the orange monarch's wings

I behold the great green & scarlet caterpillars mingling with the bodies
of those I love & my blood roars the messenger is your double name

1 October 1970, Sherman Oaks

110

In less than the pulsation of an artery it
is altered —
             where you were was suddenly
not — you stood
by her tub
her word to you
you allowed, put
you in Eden —
             you entered not
to free her, but for
company —
             knowing you were dead you wanted you
picked her up you
danced with her you
thought not of freeing her nor
yourself you
longed to get one
thing straight
             you
saw the possibility of
a poem, you
danced with her you
demanded to pick her up
(pick him up) you
demanded to speak with
the King (the
Queen) You told her
the greatest thing can
happen between us is

a child She told you (He
No, it's Us (She
actually, then: orgasm is
the best thing can happen
between us,
             jogging in Max's
Kansas City you
shouting No
it is a child She No
it is an orgasm
             You
walked her home
You walked,
her home. She
(He
walked
beside you (You
invited you're In

111

now in this filthy
(the red rags around
her (His
legs, 31
feet under ground
a little bowl placed
under the bars held
rice, you ate that thinking,
you wanted to masturbate in
her, That
She (He
said was alright (So she
ate His cock there A
servant it seemed placed
strangled by your ear
Forced jetty

the dream opened
a summer house with
all your relatives were
Grand Central Station on
the frontporch your father as
you rummaged at her
clothes, delightful moustache
40, his age when you
were born, Come on in
(at the rim of her bathtub
morning What do you do
when you are alone?
                    Why I
masturbate (entered in that word
the roundhouse of all the peoples of
the earth refracted of
course 50 prisms say, visible
reunion (stuck
with the ball & streamers, but
Then He taking you thru the Aunts
& Uncles to

Your Mother! What sweetness now!
How lovely to have life moving at
the gait of the poem! That seemed
your mother (He disappeared
sprung upon you as your life
with the other relatives (Esh
leman Little Ash Tree outside
And then my mother & I, she
now in her motherform, were in back
yard under the familytree summer
here winter Adrienne now Caryl
Our conversation is a lovely fucking
I mean my mother was a spider

We were going up & down in her
(His web She (not
how to instruct me (
blank shot the pride
blaze but that's ok
you're in the only place you'll
ever be it's personal I mean it's
sexual the tree that curves before
You just can't step outside this or
the tree is America — O
that's what you were telling me O
this tree with the bathtub in its roots
Is what happens when I walk down the street
What street your head This son is
What I wanted to tell you Adrienne
Ariadne but since you can hear me it's
not just a dream & my mother & I were
Under my voice it rolls along my feet
Thru the ground Is there a distinction
She, was asking, Do You (He
understand now We'd better go back
Daddy wonders where we are
(but the bright gladiators I cautioned
Here, you can touch it, that's
fury, you'd just better rip up that sheet
You're drunk now in the heart of the poem
But I was just walking down (He
was off talking to the relatives (The
Relatives, the Puns, What fun so I
did that little wincing walk down the aisle
splashing & splashing & splashing Was
it just you wanted to see your Father &
(Him, No I wanted (He
ah, to live a little Not to be locked out
Ah we'd better go back your Daddy's
a drunk boat roacking & roacking
ok — my pain is about done I'll die soon so
We'd better go back to Him (red rags
but is that my father a piece of shit (She
now lost under (He was talking Aunt Ivy
I mean Uncle Charles how beautiful Indiana
outside of America is (the chains on Angela
Davis like a campus lies of course you want
She's a part of you (I wonder How father did
you know her (well I had rheumatism at 18 then I
started to play the cornet O
I understand now how you feel No
wonder we're under the banister
it's ok to get inside like this without
surface, ah they're gonna be awful mad
at you talkin like this, I know Dad, but
this was how our talk was you know you

113

never spoke To me I know the poem is only
inside (He What you wanna do Split my
Head no this joke is very serious You
Must not blow up the pen
How did we get here Well you Fell
Can't we leave now No I have that old
car in which you always wanted to ride
O I thought you were Caryl no just a body you
swear fidelity now? Of course to you since
You're me sleeping but I'm awake Of
course you are you're sitting in this chair
You mean if everybody were to do this Yes
(He ho ho ho (& then Aunt Iva not Ivy but ivA
that were your grant him her You won
Jesus my father how nice to taste your seamless
Grant Get in, it's an old car a buggy won't
take us Far That's a number Get in
I just wanted to ride a while listen to my
poem sink into its manure O that's (SheWe
weewee rode along little droplets down I
just waking walked with a hardon out of sleep
What do you do when you (bumping down that
countryroad My father & I to get a beer O
yes with Robert & Denis bumping down night
but the town was closed (HeShe absolute
fern wrath overcoats the people in overcoats
They were like trees the Town
the beerhalls closed only little lights
But that's my dream my father said Just
it is Just to ride with you 60 or so years
O well I was turning to Caryl now in Adrienne
Who are they Well you can't now know Since
the Trees of Eden had on overcoats Well
it's beautiful you're out of America (O i

9 November 1970, Sherman Oaks

114

BOTTICELLI CHILDHOOD CONJUNCTION

O sing thru me, Sandro Botticelli,
  power to wed
in the mastiff uprush,

        white running thighs attacked   [Decameron V.8]
in the four panels of your painting
depicting the story of Nastagio
degli Onesti,
            unknown woman
naked running pursued by
knight on horseback,

Onesti stunned
out of dreaming, mastiffs
at her,
        to watch that apple of our eye
brought down,
            sing Botticelli how
Death dismounts
slits & wrenches from that most dear back
inmost heart,

feeds it to white
& black mastiff
I cannot feign to
discover my mother's
death here,   no metaphor
to gloss the actual
bed rails,
            yet how I desire
her still,   how I dream of her alive
nightly,

        I tear at heart,
I come to this torment
twelve years old,
her death places
me,
        I know that moment,
that dear dear moment
Sparkie gave birth to her pups

wild that at that time
I should be twelve!
To touch the miniature
whale-backs of her puppies,
dark in the garage I
sawed a hole thru,   this

is that moment to stand
by the white picket fence
yearning to part lips dreaming to
struggle out of dreaming,
How your painting begins to
fill in the story,   I see your
primavera,   total,   scattering
flowers on the world & I see
primavera also running naked
no woman is known
crashing the stillness of your thought,
pine-woods,   your hero Onesti
stunned,   hardest understanding:

    to dream in heat,

        Scylla,   hydra,   sensed
in hydrangea dreaming to
snag the apple of my eye
while this dog
was birthing again & again
behind me!
        There is a crypt of
chickenwire I place my mother in,
that moment! Place her in
imagination, drive spirit into
Menonite soil,
        I drop this carnation down
because the drill-fields of
this world are opaque lid
lavender-brocaded wood to be
sealed concrete lid, this is
breathless, the carnation in some
suck of wind slithers off, one
story in multiple form!

        O Botticelli the beauty
of that moment Onesti sees,   Eshleman
sees
    Don't meddle,   no story overlaps,
what knight beside us,
the moment of our yearning is
the moment of her death,
        There is a crypt of chickenwire
afloat on White River,   I paddle
beside it,   I am split between this crypt
& the gorgeous,   Not
"I became a poet at 12"
but   *Poor sperm nailed*
like Saint Sebastian to her

boiler insides,   to be troubled by

116

1483,   can I get
Onesti in view
her death a fraction
of art,   & art
but a stroke of green turf
compared to
her death,

            the poses! the poses!
Sparkie would come in, worm
thru the hole I had sawed,
sit by brood in night by
sleeping Nash
& whipping her
in the name of
my father's arm-stroke
because she shat
on the stepping-stones
by the front porch!

So my mother dies
& I am hit by the fact I
never saw birth
& whipped life,
under what leaves does
Onesti pose,   what a sly man
watches in the pine
of the work to trick
the work
to birth?

But there is no
jade god,   no red
windingsheet in the
source of my artifacts
for her,
            I can teach —
but the truth is
milk-saucer
meal &
rubber-jingle-bone,
I'm not buried
in Indianapolis,   but I
imagine out of
Indianapolis,
how I'd love to set
that banquet, Sandor,
lure the Traversari family to
THE spot, yes, arrange
Eshleman Reunion with ice cream &
childrens' games & into the prim
bring as magician magnificent

117

terror in   to topple
cranberries on their laps,   the tables
inward, while beauty
unknown screams a white
woman tackled by mastiffs
at their feet,   & then would
thru the Elkhart
heritage,   thru Wabash
& Wakarusa,   would
on this bridge over
the abyss,   the night flames
flickering,   in the huddled
clump of my terrified
heritage one
relative,   one person
feel the flaming bit of Goya
& acknowledge my mother's
Spanish source?

          And I wonder too,   could I
trick HIM in here?   Could I, as he
pulled out, appear to him
in her face,   or in some way
now polish the Nash bumper, the
impossible question to such tone he
would cry & walk over to the mashed
petunias where together we whipped
Sparkie & once & for all assume
the figure of the cross?

                    4 December 1970, Sherman Oaks

118

Starting in again, a glass of cold water I
toss at you beautiful hiding & laughing on my
part of the bed, you jumped into my bath I
sat on the toilet shaking with laughter while
you bathed & when my turn came
the damn water was lukewarm, as I shivered
in it only up to my crack you posed
& giggled — & so I chase you thru this poem, to
spurt cold at you again, dancing woman on
my part of the bed, figure now involved with
curtains I would hang for you to giggle &
twist over your naked stomach & breasts,
but we don't have curtains, the sunlight pours
daily in, open to green oleander & Japanese
gardener's abashment, how strange to love &
sleep before open window, embrace you & watch
human twigs or sweet stones half submerged
in mud, this house the regeneration of Japanese
house from which nature was outside, each
yellow butterbur pain, obsessed with nature
since there my nature was withheld, a glass
of cold to toss liquid flame in the energy that is
joy, hear the blue-headed birds hit pane they see
only a world opening, blue-feather smear over
king-sized bed our one possession here, light
that is tossed back & forth, tepid water I
gladly sit in adore you Queen Shebaing with
towel what a lovely embrace the light water body
on the one road with heart, what a simple
throne bed is to lie sleep & peek at you
O lovely rhythm that doesn't need myth other
than blue bird feather smear a pain coronation
head of the bed that my head can spill Protean
spermacetti without wincing since you are terminal
& again my train arrives

                   Poem that drifts down to
the boy in tub she who is dead now bathed & can I
keep the glass of cold water tossing to you who
flirt in the folds of memory, figure of lovely Caryl
you are strong enough to let this dash of water be
potato & weenie, the knotty-pine dining-room with
porthole window where the boy filled with protein did
not know an Austrian doctor had made a last judgement
to affirm love life of 12 years old, & as the cold water
tosses it is wind at the end of Boulevard Place over
untying of newspapers to trundle on my route

I know of you not unlike my vision of her, vision I tossed
in again in Japan standing on the island mid Higashiyama-
road & watched the white linens toss on second story
roofs, there an innocent beholding of my mother the
photo of her at marriage lovely the photo of my father
at marriage lovely, I copulated them in the pain of
rooted to island waiting for the streetcar to carry me
downtown Kyoto 1963, seven years, but 28 years to
suddenly not in grass but in living memory sense
them, & the boy rushes in mind to put them in love
the white flapping towels & linen, All commingling of
light & clothes the desperate first, & I rushed cold
water into that possible image, no body to be hit but
road & rode downtown, & that was the pain to have no
terminal for first sprinklings of joy

                    & so she bathed the
crack of the boy insisted I not shower not linger in
bed at morning, those covers are still warm in the bed
over which life does seem to toss, a glass of cold
can be Arctic or can be joy & I love my first imaginings
of my mother tho no net caught the fish my mind/body
is, to throw & to throw in the throe that is the poem
your body Caryl the water dribbles down, runs to
foot of the bed that runs on its rails of world from
boy to man, there is a bed, one, we always inhabit
we are born in are nursed in fuck are lonely in &
sleep, this bed primally the door we open & close,
& you Caryl swirling flesh campanile sweet leaf
risen from the bloody waves,

                  This is no myth, it is
my life & the dogs that tear at the beautiful flesh in
Botticelli while the drinkers rear from their picnic
tables in alarm are watersparkle from your body
you walk on the water I throw & I live on the water you
breathe & my mother in sunlight a halo of energy I
will have here around you, I see Gladys Eshleman
thru the halls of the golden string of imagination, I
see the thirty-five stages of my years of her life, she
is the curtains, the opaque folds we won't have in our
life, she is the backdrop my imagination loves to
see you dance against, playing at the organ & playing
pedaling the organ, pressing my feet down into deep
wood of boyhood piano scales upon scales dragon of
green Victory Stamps my little ass on the needlework
rose of piano-bench Teaching Little Fingers to
throw the glass, press down Play & learn to walk
index over third finger the endless bass somber thru
The Rustle of Spring, Revolutionary Etude ultimately
Bud Powell who swirls in the curtain of the letter,

that black woman who crossed the hospital parking-lot
as she spoke her last coherent words to me the mind
wants to make Kali, black death goddess crossing
parking-lot having laid her cancer stinger of endless
hunger in the pitiful old woman wild & nut-colored on
the bed! All I know has rushed from me protein so
Proteus may live, if there must be the shadow wch is
myth I want it that close, not have to speak death in
black attendant heavy towards her car 7 stories down
from the monolithic wings of hospital, absence of angel
angel only in the glass you have poured full & I toss
& toss this cold water wake up my mother from the
last dreadful slumber by walking in unannounced

        "oh, hello, Clayton . . ."
how much water is there in this glass, smell of pepper
tree, dried oleander flower, stand in California back
yard & know sex-economy is the energy household
sprinkle of Aquarian stars of the woman I am pouring
out, shallow pool on concrete, how much can she
pour who is pouring thru me? No way to know other
than to not fear the pouring, curtainless window is
to pour & pour & now I am upon you shielded
before the carnation bones of funeral lime-colored
Flanner & Buchannan the lavender-brocaded casket
with its heavy silver bars weight of weenies in my
plate weight of porthole window weight of the haunt
of house. I think my mother is consumed in this endless glass, treat decently this energy household this
is thy core of ecology to live in a body maybe to end
up nut, wild-child, mother as man alone in the spinal
woods of monster losing her hair, sack-cloth of cancer to
ram food at one's mouth, smear into teethless gums
a morsel of bad-smelling fish, confuse coffee-cup with
pot & see her legs the accuracy of Grünewald's vision
of the Christ, mottled & damp in sores legs that in
hose were monument by piano my fingers pressed in
& in, that this IS a casket lowered into shovel-sliced
Menonite earth, that this is the end of man over wch
rain & fog drizzle in the face of the sad Eshleman tribes,
pink rabbit-eyed faces of north Indiana women huddled
in the unending death of no one ever throwing water on
the possibility of happiness, is not this the meaning of
rain, is not this the meaning of sunlight to not let
hideous rabbit, the wild-child, park in the center of
our longing? Are not these jumpings on the mattress,
the dash to the faucet & the run after you laughing
the meaning of life? And what monument more than to
gauge her drift thru me, the satanic point at wch I
would not turn on the tap but deny the spiritual economy
keep the glass empty, which, in the strength of her wish,
would have been not to write but play out the piano into

the settled negation that is Indianapolis. O mother, it
was in Kyoto I beheld thy triple-negation at the point I
first knew you were my mother! O tonight I wld crown
that point, that you came to me there in the fury of
unacted desire & thru a spider, abdomen red &
swollen, in the heat of summer transmitted to me
Isis, that who prunes us to let creation thru seeks
likewise our scattered members, & the boy at 12
who stood by white pickets behind the garage while
great Reich was actually thinking about him in Europe,
that boy a page before the court of women attacked
by mastiffs, who stood trembling while the white
table-cloths soaked in the wine, this boy before
the overturned banquet of humanity you brought to
bear upon the suffering spider body, who could thru
such rabbit-eyed tradition manifest yourself, for
the fountain you had at least to plant, you left your
stacking of coins at least an instant to take on the
spider-body & be again the beginning of world.

7 December 1970, Sherman Oaks

THE BRIDGE AT THE MAYAN PASS

I

Five nights stone
has crowded in, to
say my father's
face is stone, to

dress his face in
the stone of
stone that speaks more
powerfully as

the father of my
father & his father
but I can only love
that which is no

more impersonal than
my seeing of
myself, & since I have
no childhood memory of

my father's face
I have been rocked to the edge
of Last Judgement, I
was moving toward

eternal fire, across the bridge
I was building of
the poem, had put on
that Mayan bridge

a hunched form, in the darkness over
the swaying pass, below us
the abyss I sought to
watch a huge wounded

shoulder of a form roll
into, Goya's Satan this Christ
I thought, & adored
the phantasmagoria of

Billy Graham in bra &
garters, like the Rhine
Gold girl, serving the
pitiful legions of Eshleman

beer, in the nave, the

elders who are
my Presbyters. But to bring
lightning here, to

smear a face, which
as A face is
His face, into stone, to
establish the gaping

cisterns of Tlaloc's eyes
as *my father's face,* my
marriage of
heaven & hell, evades

my feelings about the living
man. Tonight I remembered
a flicker, a wince
of suffering, very

quick, an instant, a
flicker stronger than stone
across the mortuary
lobby I saw, in

his face, as I turned from
the relatives who had
turned from him, & saw
him, suddenly

alone. He stood
on the bridge &
looked for me, I was
simply a wider

flicker, burning with more
hate & more love
than he, No — with no
more hate, no more

love than is here, this
bridge of ceaselessly
eroding alarm, this
bridge in a stronger

moment I call the
golden string. But the fiber of
the string is likewise creaking
wood & wind,

it holds the entire
phantasmagoria of the
weighted dread
I am & I am & I am.

II

But I refuse to contend
with *your stone!* I have been there, consciously, father, you
have not! You are in under her, the stone she lies on,
I fought with you in Vallejo, I struggled to
kill Vallejo at stone
my contention with man!
I am sick to death
of what won't stink!
Caryl is alive, Matthew
is alive, am I
alive? SICK TO DEATH
of baptism without desire,
& I know through the worm,
through the humility at odds
with woman is, the magic
of your unreadable runes!
You are the stone
a boy cannot read,
I write to make
to Matthew Matthew
visible, that a fucking
transmission be made!
But this stone ground, how
long will the indian
patch up San Cristobal his huts,
skulls, his houses, black
window eyes, eyes, a thousand
black eyes candle-lit over our
Christ-leaden city of Lima!
My god, father, you didn't even know
we were in Lima! You voting
& voting & not even knowing
lacunae
lacunae
in the indian's water-supply, in
the copper-lines that extend like
intestinal cords between here &
South America, STONE!
You didn't even know what you were doing when you fucked Gladys!
Her one erotic memory was a choir-master in Chicago who
        around 1930 looked at her!
I am angry at you because you didn't know how to fuck!
I am angry at you because having moved through the superficial
        layers of her death I do not reach the living,
but hit you! I am furious at you because you don't know what
        goes on in Lima!
I hate you because when you traveled to Lima you couldn't look
        at a starving child but went to Macchu Picchu!
FOR THAT IS THE ADORATION OF STONE!
I HATE STONE, I bring pieces of it into my room only

125

to weight the pages from the wind
on which the honest words of men who have lived through
    their lives live!
I HATE THE STONE IN MAN,
I HATE THE ADORATION
    OF YANG MARKS
    IN BUFFALO PAINTINGS
    & YIN CIRCLES BEFORE WHICH
    THE SITTING WORLD ADORES
    THE HISTORY OF MAN!
I hate you because you are simply a cruddy uninteresting piece of
    this history!
Because you would watch
    black children bring you a newspaper & not give them a Xmas tip
but would give white children a Xmas tip,
& because you would chase children away from the buckeye tree
    because they crept into the yard while I was 8 sitting back of
    the porthole window wishing I was creeping into our yard
    to steal the unquestionably free fallen buckeyes!
And so you are in me, & I feel my hate for you my mother dies!
My mother dies! Yes, complex knot of real feeling through which
    burning rivulets leaked through, her tears awakened my going-to-hell
    cheeks, & you sitting 30 years in the slaughterhouse
    creeping, your pen, across the ledger, coming home with your
    bloodstained coat tips, that I had only those rainblooddrops to
    imagine what you were drawing salary from! The nerve of you, to
    not break down ever once & WEEP with the blood of a cow
    on the heels of your Charlie McCarthy shoes! The nerve of you not
    to cry! The nerve of you never to blast me! The nerve O the NERVE
    dead, dead & dead & dead & dead *dna dead dna DEAD*
Yoru roars! Yes, the faculty that otherwise is literary careful sadness,
literary adolescence forever wrapped in the many-colored coat of myth,
what a Joseph coat you are, Ira Clayton Eshleman, & the neighbors all
picking around in the suburbs looking with flashlights for the murderer
of a girl, you do not come home father, I will not let you come home
    for home is where you'd like to flicker forever, flicker a wince or
    a sad distressed look, lacunae
lacunae, sad distressed look lacunae, lacunae honorably in Catullus
Villon lacunae in the parts of man
uttered & lost in paper-rot, but damn lacunae of what is never uttered!
    AND I WILL NOT LET YOU REMAIN STONE
    FOR STONE IS
    ANCIENT FIRE
    I HONOR ANCIENT FIRE
    FOR TOTALLY NON-CHRISTIAN REASONS
    I WOULD NOT CONSIGN YOU TO ETERNAL FIRE
The ancient fire! The ancient fire! Old fire! Anger & blessing, hate
desire, concern, sympathy intermingling, Yes, this is
under Last Judgement, old pisco taste of last judgement,
music, song be DAMNED, the raw voices on benches at 12,000 feet be
held, the ancient men are those who have no clothes! Those men be
let in, those unlit roadways, those failures of rain

126

YES I AM A BABY INCAN
I RUN THE FULL CIRCLE OF THE YANG MARKS
I SEE THE ONLY THING WORTH ADORING IS MY ART
IN WHICH THOSE I LOVE ARE NOT ABSENT
And the lure of forgiveness is
consumed in the meaning of understanding
THE MEANING OF STONE IS
IT BE FUCKED ON OVER A BED OF
DOWN EVERY SECOND DAY IN THE LIFE OF MAN
And the yang marks will be seen a movement
And the yin will be seen as movement
For the meaning of movement is the body of man & woman & child
Against rock to love & keep warm
THIS IS HISTORICAL UNDERSTANDING
And the generations of Eshleman, oh let them huddle, yes, with wine
& candles on a rope bridge over a Mayan Pass! Yes over the abyss,
the whole white spook-show like Witch Sabbath! Great black shadows,
let them pass the wine, unhuddle, let my father be among his people,
Let there be that picnic with the abyss beneath, let spastic Dean Eshleman
touch Matthew that Matthew not be confused, I open this cyst that
Matthew wander fully among these generations, let him see Iva Eshleman's
madness, THIS IS THE WEIGHT, Charles, Silvia, Orville, Leonard,
Helen, Almira, Ira, Olive, Aunt Barbara never seen from Florida,
(these are the "books"), Fern, Faye, Bob Wilmore (these in Blake's
age *Generations of Man)*, THE WEIGHT THE DREADED WEIGHT I
NOW TAKE OFF INDIANA

I RELEASE INDIANA

NAILED MILE GALED IN ANSWER

TRACED IN HEIL THY NATURN FACE!

6 - 16 December 1970, Sherman Oaks

127

VII

In Kyoto, because of my stomach pain as well as the lack of a comfortable place to sit, I began to feel the tight coil and reflex of my body as I would crouch in the benjo (the toilet room) over the porcelain trench — my position reminded me of the position of Tlatzoteotl, the Aztec goddess of childbirth and filth. The version of Tlatzoteotl I had seen portrayed her crouched with a little man emerging between her thighs, his hands held up to his shoulders and curved forward, like paws. My desire became to give birth to a figure who was "primitive" in the sense that he could participate in an interdependent circuit of being, a heroic figure of the imagination, who was not haunted, as I was then, by Nature. Those years in Kyoto the sanitation-truck would come around every few months and put its long trunk-like hose into people's benjo-pits to suck out the contents. The smell was stupendous as well as unpleasant — it was the smell of the collectivecoil, common denominator of life on, and of, earth.

Tlatzoteotl was just one of the forms that Coatlicue, a major figure in the Aztec pantheon, took on. Coatlicue was referred to as "mother of the gods" and what this meant to the Aztecs is portrayed in an awesome piece of sculpture now in the National Museum of Anthropology in Mexico City.

Watching the pregnant red spider's abdomen, where her spinnerets were, I felt my own center of power. As I would look at the spider, I would see Coatlicue, and in Coatlicue/spider I saw an urn which contained the mutilated body of a woman. This mutilated body is several things at once: she is the image of woman generational man carries in his mind which controls his contacts with the world — she is also my own father/mother, the stone I had to break up in order to release myself from Indiana.

Because I could not get inside the tiny Coatlicue/spider urn to view the mutilated body close up, I expanded the urn into a silo — which is the spiritual shape of the abyss of Indiana. According to myth, the God of War saves the woman Coatlicue from her sons and sisters who want to kill her because she got pregnant without a husband. The revelation from having entered the abyss is to discover that Coatlicue is not saved but that she herself is killed and buried in the urn and that it is her body around which the idol COATLICUE is constructed.

BRIEF HYMN TO THE BODY ELECTRIC

Persimmon on my desk
full ripe, a dusty sheen on thy
skin, only feet away from the dry yet
living silver maple, and inches
      from the red stained
chunk of jasper,   I feel thy presence
dreadful, excremental, my own stomach
a mosquito filled with blood, yet rippling
dry leaves across this garage roof
& I am standing before my white childhood
garage, full ripe, a dusty Veronica in thy
window,
            nothing is dead.   O
enormous wonder of my body
interlocked with yours!

                              24 December 1972

THE OCTOPUS DELIVERY

Indiana alters, coils

"little moon worm"

    tako

a plate of fresh octopus
at the Open Sea Sushi Bar
or just the calligraphy
on the practiced paper:

虫   worm (mushi)

     with   小   little (chisai)

虫肖   月 & moon (tsuki)

first seed
as I see it now
of the curl
baby Yorunomado playing
on a leaf, that
sperm of rebirth,
draw *tako*
obsessed
by the plump
octopus muscular & coiling
beaked horror
At one place in ocean
Tell poem how it grew, how it
grows, I groaned
in the embrace of sunlight
dewy azalea out the tiny benjo window
slatted as if out a cell
(*tako*, cell, circular
germ, I pressed
the metamorphosis of octopus
out my anus crouched over
the Okumura white porcelain
trench, how my shit lay
in coils pressed
a reunion in my mind:

Tlazolteotl
FILTH EATER
     IS
BIRTH GIVER
(the flesh cut away from her mouth
her teeth shone clenched
head thrust into sun
crouched over
dirt trench adored
at the moment the head
& paws of god's
slimy ghost is open-eyed
between her thighs —
I say I looked at my coil
fresh with the octopus' life
that is so tragic I thought
squeezed crosslegged
trying to write

               but baby
was wrong, it was I did not
want to adore my weewee
caca any longer, IT WAS.
It was not my father
I had a father
It was not my mother
I had a mother
O yes! as the sensations rose
& the succulent octopus
swallowed on a pellet of rice
began to announce itself, press
as I tried to pronounce it against
my anus — I had a mother,
a fine mother pressing so
gently, so benignly curled
whose eyes looked through my stomach
heavy-lidded & sensuous if
I could just break the cribslats of God,
that ruler bicycle-chain Eagle-badge
square & four-cornered deck
of rigidity where all the stupid
(unused) trophies neighed
to be released — four-cornered
as against the curl
deep benjo pits Not the stink
of excrement (Artaud's *crap)*
Not the linear associations
with pigpen, rational mummy
wherein the germs & seeds are looked
down upon, but the festering
deposit of the populace of
Imagumano, the collectivecoil

which when opened that every third or
fourth month was JUNGLE
(cogollo) connection, neck
of the tragic
fact you & I are, transmuted
in its very waiting, composed
in its decomposition to gleam before
imagination — O what a mother
I had, but hard & toxic
in the daddy-duality of God
I couldn't mentally break down:
Paden showed me Reich then
& the two of us
were illumined by the glowing of
Reich's seizing of the daddy-bacteria
plugged into sky & offering it to
the good octopus of the tortured
human body to eat
No system but the four-cornered
pine door ripped from the bath-
room gateway, to let the stink
into the stem of house so
whoever can breathe Mexico
when Paden showed me Reich
I remembered that pukesmell of life
in the tidal rain at night
anchored in the opened pineapple
bonneted with flies at morning
& went with the Romantic legend
which I now understand
as the Japanese octopus mermaid
coiling out of ocean affirming
sexual desire like upstart
sickness in the four-cornered head
TAKO wet brush stroke is analogue
Image of energy, the for all men
always available Divine Analogue.
I love the incredible journey
for its own screwdrivers
& vises hung like beartraps
on the inside of the image,
for what happened IS the matter
of the present compost — the lie
of synapse is to make me think
the terror could be shorter,
but the coils of time digest me
at their benign leisure,
it could not have been essentially
different because the essence is
four-cornered as well as squirmy
puckered valves aglow & traveling
in the lavender & green harbors

that swirl with blood
festering communal trench
I contacted as long ago I contacted
measles, this is the force
of the poem Occult & spread
eyes all over the octopus body
crouched there Wanting to write
Having to shit Metamorphosis
of the impossible birth To define
my Self as I breathe Each
word moved the Canal body
into the Bowel body, & when
the brown Canal Body marries
the brown Bowel body
the olfactory word is born!

27 February 1972, Sherman Oaks

I woke up pregnant by a wall
where a red spider watched me
from its web; don't forget, it
told me as I rose, that I

am pregnant too but dependent
on my web. A mobile pregnant
man I walked along the wall
& as I walked the wall began to

talk, I don't want you anymore that
now you're full of me, get
lost. But you're the father of my
state I tried to hold

it from going, but it was wide &
I was small, so wide I saw
it ran around Creation
which seemed a city

within, & I pregnant with
a little wall without. What would
you do in my place?
I began to bore

into the father of my state
but as I drilled & drilled
I found my benefactor
was deep proportionate to

my drill, while on each side of
the passageway I was making
Creation seemed to abound
When I turned to retreat

I found a woman in my way
She sat crouched in my passage
head tucked between her
knees, I tried to push her out

I tried to see her face
I couldn't budge her from the shaft
& so I joined her to
my fate by pushing her up

inside me through my recent
gate. Now under double charge
I attacked the father of my

plight, the wall gave way

I stood in Creation the air
like yolk each form like running
blood I gave way like my wall
& loosed my nature

through my thighs a woman &
a little wall attached like Siamese
twins, I could get rid of them
but she could not be

free of it. You're the father of
my yoke she cried & then
I saw her face, in Creation
each thing weds &

counterweds, no one steps on
someone's spine, I lost them here
Her face boiled orange
with fire & empty

I started to shred into the flow
but I remembered the spider's
words & so strove out
of Paradise, maintained

my womblike form. And now,
because of this, I appear
to be a man & while the spider
stays my kin

I can no longer hear its voice
except when I press my ear to
any wall & all my emptiness
shakes with awe

for I remember my father
I remember the night
he crept into my cell
& my crib ran red.

Lima 1966 — Sherman Oaks 1972

COILS

Stood by the bedside, watched her shrunk body breathing brown
monkey-like on her side, her hair moth-eaten eyes open in half
sleep, Methodist Hospital on Meridian at 16th, where I was born
out this womb June 1935 "born this day at 10:50 A.M. His
Daddy seeing him enter this old world. A Little Clayton Jr.
          [Our
dream at last realized & our prayer answered. Thank God for
it all." Once again I saw the Okumura Garden & stood in the
          [dim
morning light by the maple by the red pregnant spider's web
There *had* been a garden before, a sandbox & the white picket
fence, two gardens, three, the years warm & confusing
In the Okumura Garden I awoke from her dream for me
to be a Junior, to participate in my round of the collectivecoil
The spider was the sign of my awakening & as I studied it daily
I seemed to learn nothing, its light-green yellow-speckled red
abdomen was just more swollen every day, I stood by — in trance
as I stand by this bedside now in the trance of the mystery of
cycles, yet then as now Yorunomado was bringing me another
          [kind
of learning, not an education but an Image, not an accumulation
of particulars but a phantom layer of itself, COATLICUE,
          [Yorunomado
brought me COATLICUE, a photo of that Aztec idol. "serpent-
skirt" it meant, under the photo was written: *Mother of the Gods.*
I watched the spider & my mothering education told me I shd
learn its parts, build the poem out of observed particulars a
rational thing Yet Yorunomado had set his torch to my heart
& the fumes were smoking upward, I looked at the spider & saw
COATLICUE, I smelled a density of odor in the Okumura Gar-
          [den that
did not begin or end with my body, but COATLICUE, This
          [was the
coloration in the sign, that knowledge went to COATLICUE
          [& not in
words for the spider's anatomy. Now COATLICUE seems
          [originally
a person, not an idol but an Aztec woman the story goes, out
sweeping the desert doing penance & a feather fell from sky,
she tucked it between her stomach & her breasts, went home
& found herself pregnant. Her many sons & evil sister wanted
to kill her for this, she was terrified but the foetus spoke to
          [her saying
Do not fear; I know what I am doing. When the sons & sister
          [came
to kill her the baby lept forth fully-armed, his body painted
bright-blue, his leg slender & feathered, he killed the sons

& chopped the sister into pieces, from this time on the story
goes he is named Huitzilopochtli the God of War. I stand
before the woman & the story, I see at work in the nature of
the human an alternating rhythm of birth & birth, Coatlicue the
woman become COATLICUE 10 feet tall Ferocious Yet not
meaning to be human, but a code to divine the structure of
generation, mandala, look upon me my mother is saying &
between me & you will be a golden string, you will see in this
coiling string a meaning never fully revealed. If you fear the
                                        [cycles
you will arrest this nature, you will take a piece of it & call
It Meaning, but everything I am is meaning, who I was to you
when you played in your sandbox at 3 learning how to cover it
nightly so kitty wouldn't get in & dirty where you played,
O then how my love for you was enormous & filled with light,
shimmer of light in the leaves of my love for you, Will you call
that the limit? That my meaning? And when you held on to
white pickets at 12 & longed in your first remembered heat to
put your penis into Jeannie Woodring I began to separate from
the beech & the light in its leaves, you began to dream her into
your nature so I stood then stark in the kitchen watching you,
& what you desired was no longer my warmth infolding you
but something hotter & sharper, a torrid center of blazing
fire I could not enter, & will you see me finally in that moment?
My dream over at your birth, my life over at your heat, 47
years old, becoming more & more restrictive & thin as I placed
the plate with weenies on it before you. And in an instant my
mother moves from 47 to 72, in an instant I left her & now I see
what I left on this bed, a grin the nature of the mystery is
making at me, she is small enough now for me to carry
like a lamb in my arms, to stand in the black light of
the pasture & hold her bones & fondle her dry aged arms, her
wrist tagged with a number, *Did I do this* sweeps through
my hold with a meaning below my own meaning, am I responsible
for death, is that the source of my feeling a murderer
& knowing I am, a murderer in the collectivecoil, or is that just
abuse, all the hurts & desires acoil in my mind. No — I
did hurt you, I thought I had to be free of you. *And will you
then take that as my image?* And then I am down on my knees
crawling out from under her dining-room table onto ground
that is dry & I am speaking to you as I crawl saying Look at
what that torrid center has become, look, I am 31,000 years
                                        [old
I am standing by that fence holding on to white pickets
but look at the form that holding on has taken on, look at this
desert I am crawling on seeking water — *But I am not responsible for that,* my mother speaks, *you were down under
the table connecting your tubes to Daddy, I don't even know
what you are talking about* — No, I said, I was down under
the table cutting my tubes to father, those tubes I *can* cut,
but not my instinctual ties to you, those can only be transformed, Don't you understand that when I was standing in

the Okumura Garden watching the red spider & wondering over
COATLICUE, that I was standing before my nature, which has
everything to do with you?

　　　＊

Reached the point where imagination
became the inverse of this world, there
I took the mirage for real,
the sand as mirage, what I imagined
became real, a giant indian whore
in a stable outside of Ica was
a lick of moisture,
& before her the Greek woman
Bloomington 1965 looked like moisture
like bloody drops of hot moisture these moments
fell onto my desert *Do not take them as my image*
my mothering soul was whispering to me,
This desert is Indiana, is your state of mind
bred of Indiana. What do you see in the cracks
of mirage? I see my penis pushing toward a point of
blindly, drunkenly, when I am alone, when I exist in
red, I see a center opening & opening that I seek
Indiana bred marriage the desert again becomes real
I am back in linear time,
a work of art to make in misery but misery to be concealed
in wit & blanketing of imagination, each thought a grain The
grain in wood a swirl of thought now decomposing/composing
under my hands *This is your Last Judgement the Error to be*
consolidated then cast off Your penis is a dragon-tail Take hold
Pull your body out of Indiana is Fear your Body is what
you glimpse in that crack your Body is the code of a wholeness
of being And I hesitated, I was afraid, for I saw my contraries
　　　　　　　　　　　　　　　　　　　　　　[were
now in motion, there was no turning back, my femaleness was
preparing to be revealed, If I turned back now it wld be to live
with awareness in the state of Indiana, I saw that contradiction,
　　　　　　　　　　　　　　　　　　　　[saw
Gil Ring hammer the crucifix into his livingroom wall, saw my
　　　　　　　　　　　　　　　　　　　[art
congeal into wit & bitterness under which is religious deadness
But I feared to go on for the contraries now revolving COATLI-
　　　　　　　　　　　　　　　　　　　[CUE
within Coatlicue Coatlicue within COATLICUE in beautiful
serpentine coils had no desert beneath them, I looked into
my coils *If you go & be with woman you must see this world,*
which is the crucifixion of woman, as unreal
You must live within these coils
O mother, I cried, you are not
that weenie damnation
You are poetry YOU ARE NOT

THAT WEENIE DAMNATION IS POETRY
You are a poor dreamless spectre, that happy mother who
                                        [nursed me
You are the woman who gave up your dream when I was born
I was your dream & thus you no longer had one, conned
by an aggregate of superstition & patriarchal religious malice
into believing your function in life was generation at the expense
of human imaginative fulfillment, yet I must understand your
                                        [giving
birth to my body as a sacrifice, your nourishing me as for-
                                        [giveness,
Seeking my own soul still tied to yours I drove myself into
                                        [nightmare
to get back into a dream, nightmare the void myself an armless
                                        [worm
hurtling through my small intestine night after night in 1963
                                        [Your
face, Your searching face at the end of my coils I expected to
                                        [see
But COILS ARE BOTTOMLESS, this means, in linear time
You were never there, I "expected" to see your face seeking me
holding a candle to my anus; as long as I thought I was shit
I thought you would be there —
                        Then go forth into
a birth that is & is not your own
To enter woman is the end of nightmare self-containment
According to Indiana fucking is 6 inches in
To the imagination fucking is merely a parting of the curtains
The sun & stars shout with joy in her bottomless space

Then swiftly as in the past   [1964]
I had disemboweled myself to
arrest the suicidal heart of Indiana,
I now sealed off my stomach &
sought out — rolled out of the bunk bed   [1966]
in Blackburn's workroom & said ok
Paul, I'll go with you to "Max's Kansas City"
who knows, maybe I'll meet someone there.
In the very same moment as in the past
I had thwarted my own spinning in
apprenticework to Origin I now with only   [1963-65]
(yet what an only!) a golden string spun out
of my solar plexus released myself into   [1970]
the mirage which yawned an abyss below
the drunk horde of Eshlemans on
the rope-bridge over the Mayan Pass!

A bloodstone-lined vault it appeared
immense, cistern-shaped, I floated a tiny sky-diver
against night, *Poppi how can you*
FLY? Matthew called up to me, *I am not flying!* I called
down to him, *I am falling!* But here you must not

141

dream the mothering soul was speaking, here you are
dreaming yet here you must rudder your dream —
But must I exclude the giving myself over to
hearing Matthew in my dream I returned, You told me
everything I am is meaning, How can there be a command
while I float down into the abyss? You have transformed me to
a great extent, it spoke, I am no longer your mother, nor your
soul, I am your meaning now traveling at your side
As you have evolved me *you* must evolve — you still seek to
remember Matthew, to hear in the poem his cry
Memory punctures the closed-circuit of vision

Then as suddenly I was standing again, in the bottom
of a vast place, in a muck up to my knees, which I recognized
as silage, that I was at the bottom of a silo wch was the imagin-
                                        [ative
shape of the Abyss of Indiana, an urn crossed my mind, Was
                                        [this
the place I was to bury Gladys Eshleman?

walked a little, felt the wall Almost pitch black
a little light from somewhere. mossy, crumbly. fecund-
odor. found a door More than one? shd I open
it? no handle, felt like pine
sealed in the silo-side. I turned around leaned against
it played with myself quickly got it hard
came &
the door gave, tumbled into a big room
Hadn't been noticed, so I crouched
& began to shit while I watched what was going on —
A movie was being shown, sounded like 8 mm.
a little home movie screen, title came on "Coatlicue"
like a classroom film, There was an indian woman with a broom
sweeping on aha! the desert — sad look in her face Now
a feather turning in sky falling She picks it up
hmm that's a nice feather Think I'll take it home
Well I think I've seen this movie before so I looked around
Cldn't see the ceiling, a temple feeling, fire-smoke,
off to the side of the screen a bunch of men in little slave skirts
building something. looked like
— then I saw the urn. They had an urn about 4 feet tall
2 feet wide, placed it on a rock. written on the urn's side
in chalky-blue letters the word AURA — Some more men were
bringing something to it, were carrying (& I looked back to
the screen, then to them — the body of Coatlicue (but the myth
said Huitzilopochtli was born. I thought Coatlicue went free
But no it WAS Coatlicue's body they were carrying & was she
a mess. bloody, eyes out. they broke each of her arms, then
each of her legs & wedged her into AURA. A couple smoked
Then more men came in out of the silo-side, two carrying
something looked like a small wet sheet, they turtle-necked it
down over AURA, it looked like Coatlicue's flayed torso-

                                                            [skin
flat meatless tits hanging over the chalky letters, more men
coming in, all in those funny little skirts, some bearing long
quetzal feathers, one had an enormous pair of eagle-feet which
he placed before the urn. Another slave made two cigarette
burns in the insteps so it looked as if there were eyes in the
                                                    [insteps
Other slaves were now walking back & forth swinging smoking
braziers Hard to see, vomit-perfumy, They were fitting the
                                            [eagle-feet
in under the dressed-urn, bundling the quetzal-feathers together
for legs, another slave carried in a huge fat dead rattlesnake,
the head & about 4 feet of length; they fitted this between the legs,
made it look as if it were drooping down out of the urn (like a
                                            [tube
it struck me), head between eagle-feet, mouth open Now more
                                            [slaves
with a mess of writhing little rattlers, these they arranged
                                        [around
the bottom of the dressed-urn, a skirt More slaves Two with
                                    [heavy
belt beaded alternately severed-hands ripped-out-hearts, draped
this "necklace" around the "shoulders" of the dressed-urn.
                                        [Two
chunks of stone were fixed to the dressed-urn-shoulders,
severed rattler-heads, open-fanged, to the stones. Generation
now nearly complete, with these rattler-forearm-outleaps,
was thatch-marked all over by several slaves with knives &
in each thatch-frame a peyote-bud was impressed; the slaves
moved back as if to admire their work. Two shadowy forms
                                        [lifted
out the urn-mouth, two big rattler heads, neck-bodies arching
out backwards while they faced inward — then closed like sliding
doors Kissed & Froze making A head which spoke

Huitzilopochtli's Vision

Out of your mother jealousy &
out of your mortal fear I will rise

many-armed, I will involute & grow
a self-contained dread so vulnerable
they will murder you &
worship you, I will teach

worship of your murder
through that most silent
thing stone, one little fear
watered daily thru ritual

is eighty-foot dolmen families
on knee tremble before

COATLICUE I will build, but will
not explain it is a code; instead

I will call woman mother, I will cut
down into her chest, sink a uterus
into her stomach thus mitigating
her solar fire, Woman is dirty

I will propose, because she is
bloody with my own idea of death.
I will thus recircuit
the cathedral of her vagina

into a slaughterhouse where

hungry foetuses exchange baton,
I will manufacture perfumes out of
her pulverized cathedral to dab
on her bloody gate, men will hate

this place yet they will be insanely
drawn to it, it will appear telluric &
magnetic, the cohesive madness of
society, against which men

will rush or debate or ponder off in
ashrams while others, given up,
will live in dark shacks & dream —
But not just dream, they too

will be busy, breaking their foetuses
in, lighting incense, girding
themselves for war, delighting
in symbolic acts, bayonet-lunge,

yet insisting these acts are not
symbolic, but *natural* to man.
And my victims, where are they?
O where are you, victims, cowering

in your dark stained Peruvian colors
inwrapped against the sunset in rose
& dirty crimson filthy black greasy
scarlet, O souls of women Why

do you hang back in the dark migraine
stables, why do you not organize
forth, come forth in your righteous
cause, come fully forth with your en-

cumbering uteri, your bothersome chest-
weights, come forth into my ax-work.

144

Until my generational throne is under-cut
by mutual vision of regeneration

women will wander out on the road at
night animal-souls before my beaming eyes,
for my car is not armor, but an alembic
in which a girl is gang-fucked,

dear old Plymouth dirty backseat,
dear beer-cans on the floor,
hair-grease-smudged window
you make her real, dear

crammed butt-tray, oil-smell
O empty front-seat, cracked
rear-view mirror, I glance &
see Tenochtitlan, contrary

of Indianapolis white wash,
a few yards away the Sons of the Sepik-
Delta smoke & piss &
joke, secretly they want to all

cram into her cunt together & there   — the projector
blow themselves apart,   was turned off.
To die In a paradise   The slaves
They can Foul — millions   started cleaning up
                                           Pretty soon
arranged in stadium hypnotized   everything
by an oval where ants   had been
represent them — I will distort   removed
energy thus & raise a priesthood   except
                                           the internal
to enforce & weekly meet in   structure
worship of mutilated human being   they'd
                                             created

                    *

I turned to Yorunomado now by me by my mother's bed —
I asked him to assimilate her body, that she be buried at
the center of my poetry; yet thru his eyes I saw her alive &
                              [fine,
around 50, sitting up in bed, with a pitcher of wine on her
                              [night-table,
She offered me wine from her bed, passing me a glass of it
as I left, looked into it, then ran! the bodies of numberless
dead, The burgundy, Yorunomado spoke, is loaded, a piece of
her placenta is stuck inside you. Go back to the 59th line of
Huitzilopochtli's Vision — you are still desiring your mother,
thus I cannot assimilate her. The wine you take from her is
                              [afloat

145

with bees & flies, a brew, not a wine; a witch is still alive in
your mind. I flew back to the 59th line, found the Plymouth still
parked off 86th Street in the woods behind the golf-course, my
teen-age werefriends milling around while one by one we took
turns inside. I could not immediately understand why
this scene was stillborn in my mind. There must be a total
transformation, Yorunomado said — there is something
in your present life keeping this scene intact. As long as it
remains intact you will dream your mother is alive. And as
                                        [long
as she is alive I cannot receive her. I think I know where this
                                        [leads,
I told him, why you have brought me again to fall 1950
Indianapolis, for as I look at this Plymouth I see another car,
a Volkswagen Caryl & I rented a Sunday the spring of 1970,
drove to Harriman State Park & ate acid in the woods. Filled
with that poison I began to shout for Hollie, my "new" Marie,
the person I had chosen, after meeting Caryl, to love, but love
as self-torture. Before Caryl I was screaming for Hollie —
why are you not here? Up to that time I had responded to Caryl
only with my body; in my mind I still saw woman *femme fatal*
on one hand, housewife on the other. Caryl & I came back to
the car at dusk, parking-lot filled with picnicing Puerto-Ricans.
Caryl had her camera, we started taking pictures of each other
over the back of the Volkswagen — once looking thru the lens
I saw Caryl — saw *Caryl* — not La Muerte nor a slave
but an exasperated sweating angry woman who was original!
She was not the image of woman I had absorbed in my mind.
She was not superficial, she was fresh.
At that moment I felt my woman image divide, & fall
to the ground, a broken mask — yet in that very moment something in me refused to fully be with Caryl. I still had a piece
of need to hurt her, to be almost totally with her but not quite,
& thus the dream you Yorunomado picked up a moment ago
in this vision, the shadow moving a 50 year old mother
up in bed was my fantasy of the "beautiful Mokpo" I
could sneak off & fuck when I have no sexual need to. In the
composition of my mind that Mokpo stands for what of Indiana
still clings in me, the ritual tendency to destroy what I have
achieved, a composite that includes hurting who I most love,
projecting itself on a woman, seeing woman as "dark" opposed
to its own "light," making woman repository for the fuel it
                                        [needs to
keep itself alive. Although I do not live with a statue of
                                        [COATLICUE
this stone of religion is present. I now understand that the
                                        [forces in
my own life I must oppose to keep on learning are not a woman.
Yorunomado's eyes were gleaming & he smiled at me, he
smiled at me like no one has ever smiled at me in my life;
he turned his magnificent black New Guinea headhunter head
toward the Plymouth where I beheld the most marvelous thing:

146

I had buried my mother. Niemonjima was present. The soft
chrysalis split a lovely golden slit, her slimy infant shape
weak at first clung to her husk, slowly an iris her wet
obsidian-tipped wings unfolded turquoise & gold, scarlet
& deep green, wavered then taking off a ripple running thru
the whole of creation lifting into the glowing azure sky over
the intense Okumura Garden where I stood amazed watching my
image separate from me, & by the persimmon where stretched
the pregnant red spider's web Caryl appeared, I love
you I cried, I love you with all my life, you are Caryl
& you are what counts. With you, in you, through you I explore
the ever-returning virginity, which is freshness most of all,
repeatable & repeatable, biological light in love with imagin-
                                        [ative
light, your light to respond to my darkness, my light to res-
                                        [pond
to your darkness. I love you as a man & as an imagination —
the sacrifice poetry demands is not abstinence nor a shedding
of personality but the sharing of one's penis or one's vagina
with the cornucopia of the ages while one takes in disembowel-
                                        [ment
& emanates silk. The beloved who is true, the lover who is
                                        [true,
do not disembowel each other, yet both love each other & are
thus open to the world which is obsidian to the virginal body of
love; yet the world is also a perceptive field ever-widening to
an awakened person. I love you is my happiness with you &
at the same time a vibration sent forth against the opacity
clogged in my body & mind against this flowing persimmon.

        Yorunomado closed the left half of my book.
        From this point on, he said,
        your work leads on into the earth.

                30 March — 18 September, 1972
                Sherman Oaks.

147

Printed February 1973 in Santa Barbara for
the Black Sparrow Press by Noel Young.
Design by Barbara Martin. This edition
is published in paper wrappers; there
are 200 hardcover copies numbered & signed
by the poet; & 26 lettered copies
handbound in boards by Earle Gray,
signed & with an original holograph
poem by the poet.

CLAYTON ESHLEMAN was born June 1, 1935 in Indianapolis, Indiana. He attended Indiana University where he received his A.B. in Philosophy in 1958 and his M.A.T. in English Literature in 1961. From 1961 until 1964 he lived in the Far East, mainly Kyoto, Japan. In 1965 he spent a year in Lima, Peru, completing his translation of César Vallejo's *Poemas Humanos*. He moved to New York City in 1966, where in 1967 he began *Caterpillar* magazine which is presently in its 19th issue. In 1970 he moved to Sherman Oaks, California, and taught for two years at the California Institute of the Arts. He presently lives in Sherman Oaks where he is completing a prose work called *Heaven-Bands* and a translation of Vallejo's *España, Aparta de mi este Cáliz*.